The Storyteller

Tales of Stories and Dreams

by

John Lamendola

DORRANCE PUBLISHING CO., INC.
PITTSBURGH, PENNSYLVANIA 15222

ISBN # 0-8059-4482-6
Printed in the United States of America

First Printing

For information or to order additional books, please write:
Dorrance Publishing Co., Inc.
643 Smithfield Street
Pittsburgh, Pennsylvania 15222
U.S.A.

I had a vision of you watching me write my stories.

Dedicated in loving memory of my mother, Mary Lamendola: Born April 9, 1926; Died June 7, 1994.

May she rest in peace.

Dedicated in memory of my two huskies; my pride, my joy, my friends.

Rocky
Born August 15, 1978
Died December 11, 1992

Star
Born October 12, 1978
Died January, 1992

There will be a time when we play again.

Stars

In the beginning the Lord went to work creating Earth. This was one of many worlds he had created from his mind and vision. As the Lord's spirit floated above the Earth, he first created the soil, then the skies and the oceans. He created everything except man; that was yet to come. In the heavens above he created stars—not many, though, just a handful. In the Lord's mind he thought that as people began to shape up on Earth, the goodness of those with pure hearts would shine throughout time as stars in the sky when their lives ended. Animals would also become stars.

Thousands and thousands of years passed by, and the promise of life was being fulfilled. It was now the time when dinosaurs rule the earth. As certain beasts died, a light could be seen leaving their bodies. The light went upward toward the heavens. When it reached its place, it became even brighter, expanding for miles, becoming a star. Over the years the dinosaurs filled part of the heavens with stars. Over many more years life expanded all across the earth. The earth was covered with men , women, land animals, birds, and millions of species of sea life.

In the mountains a man named David watched his sheep as he played his flute. He heard the sound of an animal crying in pain. He got up and walked a short distance to where the sound seemed to be coming from, and there lay a lion, its paw bleeding. David ripped a piece of cloth from his robe and tied it around the injured paw to stop the bleeding. The lion just looked at David. It didn't make a move to hurt David. "It's all right. I think you are going to make it," David says to the lion.

Most people would not think to help a wild animal in need, but without thinking of the danger, David had gone to help an animal in need; for this David would have his place among the stars. The lion would as well, for being wise enough to recognize help and for having the knowledge not to fear. Throughout the years many flashes of light left the earth to find their destination in the heavens.

In the tenth century a woman named Camille did what she could to help children who are blind or who have other medical problems. She tried to make life a little better for these children in a time when the knowledge of medicine was very limited. Camille did everything she can think of; she cared for them and wrote stories to read to them. In the Lord's eyes there would surely be a place for her in the sky in full brightness.

By the fourteen century the stars were truly filling the heavens. Every once in a while a flash of light left the sea, as a whale, dolphin, or other type of marine animal made its way to the heavens above. Other breeds of animals made their way also, and they too filled the sky with stars and beauty.

1

In a time close to the fifteenth century, there was a man named Jason. Jason devoted his whole life to music, good and pure music, and he traveled around playing his songs for anyone who wanted to hear them. Women and children loved Jason's music, and Jason was happy to do anything he could to make life a little better during a hard time and for this Jason would also have a place in the heavens.

As the Lord looked around his universe, he told his angels that he was pleased but that there was still room for more stars in the heavens. The angels agreed but told him that it would still take more time.

During the sixteenth century, a woman named Annie, a good person at heart, spent her time cooking for those who were hungry, weak, or in need. People could come, have a good meal, and be on their way. She even tried to do what she could for animals. What a saint Annie was turning out to be! Even the king's guards stopped every once in a while to have a good home-cooked meal. Small children always hung around to eat. They didn't have anybody except Annie. She would truly be blessed and would have her place in the heavens of stars.

During the same century there was a man named John. He was a good carpenter and tried to help people who needed it. The only thing he asked for in return was a good hot meal. He could do anything as long as it had to do with building. He was a strong-minded man of goodness, and he too would have his place in the heavens. Once again these flashes of light left the seas and the earth, and the heavens continue to fill with stars of goodness.

In the seventeenth century, when the heavens were beginning to look brighter then ever before, there lived a woman named Dana. She was a school teacher. She had no family herself, so she took a personal interest in each child. She was a good teacher and filled the children's minds with knowledge. She was also a good example for the children and showed them the right way to live. She taught them to be honest, sharing, and caring, and to have honor for the world they lived in. She took the children on many picnics and always tried to teach them to respect everything in nature. She knew that by teaching them this, the world would be a better place for generations to come. Dana would also have her spot in the heavens as a star.

In the eighteenth century the world was shaping up really fast. The flashes of light were leaving by the hundreds. A good-hearted man named Gary had an idea. He wanted to start a home for children who were in need. He went to his government and told them his idea. He told them they couldn't just let it go but they must do something about it. After he explained his plan, they began to like it. They told him they were proud of him and that they would help him. When the time came, Gary would find his way to the heavens.

In the same century a woman named Sarah lived. She was a nurse, and what she did for soldiers is breathtaking. Even during battle she was ready to help. It did not matter to her what side somebody was on. To her a boy who was hurt was a boy she would try to help. "Now there is a good woman with a pure heart," said a captain to a major.

"Yes sir. She goes fast like the wind," said the major.

"That's a smart answer," said the captain.

In the eyes of the Lord, even though he can never accept war, Sarah would have her place among the stars.

On a clear night in the nineteenth century there were more stars than ever before. A woman named Jane, a very smart scientist looked for the cures to many diseases, especially diseases that affected the young. This woman worked around the clock many days and nights because she felt that these children's suffering should be stopped. She was hoping that one day she would have the breakthrough she had been searching for. She was determined because in her heart she felt the pain and sadness of the children who were suffering then. Although Jane spent her years in research, she made little progress, but for her determination and caring she would have her place in the heavens as a star. Meanwhile, many flashes of light were leaving the earth and heading for the sky.

In 1982 a professor, a very wise man of sixty-three-years-of-age had been studying the stars for forty-five years. He knew that many new stars appeared in the sky all the time. He knew that something strange was there, but he just could not put a handle on it. He knew it was something good, and he visited top officials with his theory and his figures, but they kept telling him that it was just new worlds or maybe suns. He knew, however, that there was something else happening with the beautiful stars. Two days before his death he was looking through his telescope, and he saw a flash of light leave the earth's surface and head for the sky. When it reached its destination in the sky, its light expanded for miles, and then it became a star. The man smiled, amazed. When he dies, he too will become a star for his years of dedication to finding the truth. As the years pass, many brilliant flashes of light can be seen leaving the earth and heading toward the sky.

Tales of a Haunted House:
The Return of Lou Wind

In an alley three men broke out their hammers and crowbars. The light in the alley could've been better. As it was, it was hard to see—or be seen. Their plan was to break the wall of the jewelry store to get inside. They would have tried to disable the alarm, if they had known of its existence.

The three men were known as the Rainbow Boys. Bob was a white man, Willie was a black man, and Frank was Oriental. Meanwhile Lou was sitting at home munching on Cracker Jacks when a special report came on the news. Three men had robbed a jewelry store and had taken a large number of gems and diamonds. The police named the Rainbow Boys as primary suspects.

The Rainbow Boys had found a place to hide the jewels until the search cooled.

Behind a broken-down house on the east side of town was a black lagoon. The Rainbow Boys hid the bag of jewels under a rock near the lagoon and left. All of a sudden bubbles came up from the lagoon, and the Creature from the Black Lagoon reached out, grabbed the bag under the water with him.

Back at Lou's house he was looking at pictures Greta had taken of him when he heard pounding at his door. "Who's banging on my timber?" Lou yelled.

"A letter, sir."

Lou opened the door.

"Here you go, sir." The boy waited.

Lou went and got the prize from his box of Cracker Jacks. "Here you go," Lou said as he handed it to the boy.

"Geez! Thanks a lot," the boy said sarcastically. Then he walked away muttering something under his breath.

Lou opened the letter. It was from a lawyer stating that his grandmother just died and that she had left her house to him. There was another letter. It was from his grandmother, telling him about her three cartoon friends. In her letter she said, "It seems to run in the family, and I want you to take of them."

Lou called his girlfriend at work. "Pack your bags, Greta," he told her. Then he explained to her about the letters. When they hung up, Greta said to herself, *What a man my Lou is!*

Later, on their way to the house, Lou began telling Greta about his grandmother. Then he said to her, "Now that we have a house, maybe we can start living together. I have money so we can get it fixed up."

Greta could hardly believe it, so she got her Juicy Fruits and started eating them. "Upstate Oregon is so beautiful! Lou, what's the name of the street?"

"Lagoon Place," Lou told her.

When they arrived at the house, Greta said, "I like it, Lou." Lou just stood there in eerie silence. After a minute he got out his keys and opened the front door. As they entered the front room, they saw many paintings. They looked more closely at them, and Lou said, "I can't believe it. I wonder who painted them?"

A mummy was on the right, on the left was the Invisible Man, and straight in front of them, with his hands on their shoulders, was the Creature from the Black Lagoon. Sitting in front on him was Lou's grandmother, smoking a pipe. Lou turns to Greta, "This house is eerie–like those cartoons in the picture."

They went back out to get their bags from the car, Greta said to Lou, "You know, Lou, we're the only people who can see cartoons. Ever since I met you, that's been the reason that you were my man."

"Wait," Lou said as he ran back over to the car. "I don't want to forget my Cracker Jacks!"

They returned to the house and got themselves comfortable. Lou lit a cigarette and began to inhale when his cigarette mysteriously started floating up into the air. Lou looked up and said, "You're the Invisible Man!"

"Right, Lou. Your grandmother told us about you. She was a grand old lady."

"Greta, come in here! I want you to meet somebody!" Lou called out.

Greta came into the room. She looked at the spot where the invisible man must have been and said, "Oh, yes! I've seen your picture. Lou, he's a handsome man."

"You can see him?" Lou asked, looking at her kind of strangely.

"No, I can tell where he is by his voice," she explained to him. Then the Invisible Man said, "I want you guys to meet the mummy and the creature now."

"You guys look really great," Lou said to them.

"Your grandmother was an angel," the mummy said.

"She was a real saint," added the creature.

The mummy asked Greta if she would go to the store and pick up some bandages.

"No problem, mum," she answered. During her trip to the store, the creature told Lou about the three men who had hidden the jewels near the lagoon "I took them under water with me," he told them, "but they are safe."

"These three guys–are they the Rainbow Boys?" Lou asked.

"They are thieves," said the Invisible Man, "and they'll be back."

"We have to be ready," said the mummy.

"Maybe you should wear some clothes, so that we can see you," Lou said to the Invisible Man.

Just then, Greta returned from the store. "Here are your bandages," she said, handing them to the mummy.

The mummy took them and ran right up the stairs with them.

"What was that all about?" Lou asked.

"It's something that he likes to do," the creature told them.

Lou reached into his pocket to get some Cracker Jacks when he heard a car pull up. The creature looked out the window. "It's the Rainbow Boys!"

"Come with me, I know a hiding place!" the mummy told them.

They watched as the Rainbow Boys went back to the lagoon. "They're not here!" Frank said angrily.

"What do you mean? We're the only ones who knew they were here!" one of the others said. After a minute they were all fighting with each other.

Bob tried to calm them down and make some plans. "Let's search the house. Willie, you go in the front. Frank, you go to the back door, and I'll go down to the cellar." All three men had black eyes from the fight.

Meanwhile Lou went with the Invisible Man, Greta went with the mummy, and the creature was by himself.

Willie opened the front door and started looking at the pictures on the wall. Rubbing his head, he said to himself, *Very strange.* He went up the stairs and saw a big stained-glass window. He turned to see the mummy coming out, bent over. Then the mummy blew so powerfully that the force of his breath sent Willie through the window and out onto the dying grass.

Meanwhile Greta was getting two pails of glue, and two pails of Juicy Fruits. Bob was in the cellar.

Willie came back into the house and went up to the bathroom and looked in the mirror. His hair was standing up on end, and so were his eyebrows.

Just then the mummy walked in and asked, "May I get my bandages from the shelf, please?"

Willie got so scared that he jumped through the bathroom window and landed on a bunch of thorns outside. He ran around back and waded into the lagoon. The creature from the black lagoon picked him up and threw him into the air. He landed in a tree, and there he hung with his pants down.

Lou and Greta were ready to surprise Bob. Lou came out and gave Bob a good punch, sending him to the floor. Greta got the pail of glue and threw it all over Bob, and Lou grabbed the pail of Juicy Fruits and threw them on him too. What a sight he was!

Lou locked Bob up in one of the rooms and went around back. He saw Willie hanging from the tree. "Hold on, I'll get a ladder!" Lou called to him.

After he came back with the ladder, he helped Willie down. "Look at you!" he said and then gave him a good belt. Then he locked him up in the same room as Bob.

"Oh, my Lou! What a man!" Greta said as she watched the whole thing.

Frank went in through the back door and stopped in the bathroom. Just as he was about to sit down, the Invisible Man lit up a cigarette and said, "Careful, there is a man working down there!"

Frank went right through the wall! Then the creature set a board on the floor that would send Frank right through the roof when he stepped on it. Less than a minute later Frank's head was sticking out the top of the house. So they helped him down and put him with the others.

"You better go get the police," Lou told Greta. She got in the car and took off, thinking how much easier it would've been if they had had a telephone.

Somehow the Rainbow Boys got out of the locked room and pulled a gun on Lou and three friends. "I will fight the three of you," Lou proposed, and if you win, I'll tell you where the jewels are." They agreed.

"You can do it, Lou! Give 'em hell, Lou!" his friends cheered.

"I am Lou Wind. I can do it!" Lou said.

The fight began. Lou got the three guys close together and picked up all three with one hand and slapped them silly. "That a boy, Lou! Your grandmother would be proud of you!" the creature called out, while the Invisible Man lay on his back, smoking a cigarette.

Lou threw the Rainbow Boys against a wall and knocked them out. The Invisible Man went to get some rope to tie them up with. The creature went to the lagoon, jumped in, and retrieved the bag of jewels on top of them, and waited for the police.

"It's better that the police not see us," Lou's friends said to him. Greta got back with the police, and they couldn't believe it. You're a hero, Lou Wind!" they told him. Greta was looking at her man while she ate her Juicy Fruits.

The Rainbow Boys were really going nuts.

"Now they're seeing monsters!" said one of the police officers.

"All right, boys. Take 'em away!"

Lou turned to Greta and said, "How about tying the knot?"

Greta nearly went into a state of shock. "Yes, Lou! Oh my Lou!" she said. Lou kind of shook his head with a smile, in between bites of Cracker Jacks.

Their friends came back out, and everyone was so happy.

"Lou, will you come to see us?" asked the mummy.

"I shall be back. The house is yours, as long as I own it. It will never be torn down."

"We have three other friends that would love to live here, Lou." said the creature.

Anything, guys." Lou said. "My grandmother would have been pleased."

So the creature called out to his friends–Wolfman, Frankenstein, and Count Dracula.

"Thanks a lot, Lou," they said to him.

"No problem, guys," Lou told them.

Lou and Greta drove away as everybody waved good-bye. Greta was still in shock about what Lou had asked her. "Why don't we just live there, Lou?"

"Is that what you want?"

"Yes, Lou."

"Okay," said Lou, and he turned around and went back to 3 Lagoon Place.

Mr. Lonely

John Brooks was an outstanding cartoon artist for his company. All of the other employees thought John was a great guy. It was not just for his impressive talent, but he was also kind and polite and possessed a certain charm. John always kept it deep down inside him just how lonely he was. John was thirty-nine years old, about six feet tall, and had black hair with a bit of gray at the edges.

John was planning to move to Maine, where he was having a house built and intended to start doing his work from there. The construction was moving quickly, and it looked as though it would be finished in about three months.

One day John was sitting at his desk laying out pages of his characters, when Joan Davis, an editor for the company, came in. "Hello, you must be John Brooks," she said.

"Yes, that's me. What can I do for you?" John asked her.

"Mr. Brooks, it's very nice to meet you. I've enjoyed your work for years. You're an extremely talented artist."

"Well, I thank you for that," John said, his happiness clearly showing in his eyes.

"Are you working on a new layout, Mr. Brooks?" Joan asked.

"Yes, I am, and won't you please call me John?"

"I'd love to read it sometime, John."

"Would you, maybe, if you don't have other plans, like to go to lunch? Unless there's a problem. . . ." John asked hesitantly.

"No problem at all. I would love to."

"Perfect," said John. "Just let me get my coat, and we'll be off."

As they walked to the door, John told his co-workers that he would be back in two hours. After the doors shut behind them, the other employees chattered excitedly. One said, "Well I don't believe my eyes! John is going out!"

"Amazing!" said another. "In all of the years I have worked here, I've never seen John go out. It's a good thing, though. I was starting to get worried. Sooner or later, the loneliness would have to catch up with him."

Meanwhile John and Joan had found a cozy little restaurant. "So how long have you been a cartoon artist?" Joan asked him.

"For nineteen years," John told her.

"Well, that's a long time, but how old are you?"

"Oh, I'm thirty-nine," John said. "And you?"

"Well," said Joan, smiling, "you really shouldn't ask a woman her age."

"That's true. I think I'm a little out of date," John said apologetically.

"No, you're not. I'm thirty-two."

"Okay. How's your lunch?"

"Very good," she said, looking very closely at John. John looked at his watch quickly. "I'm going to have to get back to the office," he said. As they stood from their chairs, John said, "I had a wonderful time."

"So did I. I was wondering, my sister is having a get-together tomorrow evening. Would you like to come?"

"Yes," John said. "That would be a real treat."

"Great," said Joan. She took a minute to write her address and phone number on a scrap of paper and handed it to John.

"I'll see you then," she said.

"Okay, then," said John as he headed back to his office. When he got back to work, the other employees noticed that he looked really happy. "Did you see how happy he looked?" said one.

"You know," said another, "I haven't seen him that happy since I started working here, and I've been here nine years!"

When John got home, his dog, Buck, started jumping all over him. He was a beautiful great Dane. "Okay, boy, okay. I'm home," John said. I've got good news. Tomorrow night I'm going on a date." Buck just looked at him.

"What do you think of that?" he said, then went over to the window and shouted, "New York, I have a date."

"He closed the window and smiled to himself. "Goodnight, Buck," John said, going into his bedroom.

The next day John left work early so that he could buy some new clothes. He also stopped by a florist and picked up some flowers to give to Joan.

That night as John got to the front door, he looked at himself and thought, *Not Bad.*

He rang the doorbell, and Joan answered the door. "Hello, John," she said.

"Hi. These flowers are for you," he told her.

"Oh, they smell great," she said as she put her nose to the flowers. She looked at John with a bright smile. As they got to John's Jeep, John opened the door for Joan and helped her in.

"You look very nice tonight, Joan," Joan told him.

"Thank you. You look outstanding."

When they got to the party, Joan said to her sister, "Rose, there is someone I want you to meet. This is John Brooks. John, this is my sister, Rose."

"Pleased to meet you," John said to Rose.

"Would you like a drink, John?" Joan asked him.

"Yes, please. A glass of white wine would be great.

Throughout the party John and Joan spent their time together talking. John tried to tell Joan about some of his problems. He told her how all of his life he had been in a sort of shell and that it seemed like he was always alone.

9

"You've never been married?" Joan asked.

"No, have you?"

"No," Joan said, giving him a quick kiss. "Maybe we can get you out of your shell."

John smiled at her and felt hopeful. Joan smiled back at him. Their eyes never left each other.

Standing with her husband, Rose watched John and Joan from a distance. "Would you look at that! They haven't taken their eyes off each other!"

Joan and John soon left the party. John took Joan home, but when they got there, they did not go inside. They sat on the steps and began to talk about everything that was important to them. John told her about how much he loved Maine and that he was having his dream house built there.

"Oh, how nice, John! I would love to see it sometime," Joan exclaimed.

"Well," said John, "how about this weekend you and I take a ride up there?"

"That would be wonderful! Can we talk about it more over dinner tomorrow night?"

"I will see you tomorrow night then," John said. He kissed her goodnight and headed for his Jeep.

As he was opening the door, Joan ran up to him and kissed him again, "Goodnight, John," she said. He watched her as she ran back to the house. He felt happier than ever before in his life.

The next day at work all the other employees noticed how happy John seemed. In the afternoon his boss came into his office to drop off some papers, "Hey John, how is everything? I heard that things are looking pretty good for you lately."

"You know," John said, "They really are." He smiled.

"I am happy for you. I don't know a guy who deserves it more than you. See you later, John."

"Later, boss," John said as he got back to work. He was in a great mood throughout the day.

Later that night Joan and John met at a fine restaurant for dinner. "I would like to make a toast. I am not really very good at this, but here goes," John said. "I want to make a toast to our happiness: May we always feel as we do right now and may our lives always be filled with the joy love brings, now and forever." They lifted their glasses into the air and touched them together.

"That was so wonderful, John!" Joan said, smiling. "I loved it," and she took his hand.

"Well, I guess it wasn't that bad," he said.

"Oh, it was perfect," Joan said, and she seductively slid her foot up and down his leg.

The rest of the week was complete happiness for them both. They went to a Broadway showing of *Phantom of the Opera*, they rode through Central Park in a carriage, and they topped it off with ice cream at one of the local parlors.

Finally the day to go to Maine came. They packed their bags into John's Jeep and set off.

When they arrived at the hotel, John said to Joan, "How are we going to do this?"

Joan smiled at him. "Just get one hotel room," she said and smiled, looking him up and down.

They left the hotel and went to see the house. When they arrived, Joan was amazed. "Oh, how wonderful!" she said. "Look at the sun deck, and the rooms are outstanding!"

"Yes, but it won't really be finished until it is decorated, and I am not sure just how to do it."

"Oh, John, would you let me do it? Would you?"

John smiled. "Do you really want to?" he asked. "That would make me very happy."

Joan threw her arms around John and gave him a kiss. Later they went to dinner, and they could not stop kissing and holding hands. After dinner they headed back to their hotel room.

Joan took off her jacket and said, "John, do you think you could go and get some wine, and maybe some cheese?"

"Of course. I'll be back in a few minutes."

Joan set out a bucket of ice for the wine and went into the bathroom to take a shower.

When John got back to the room, Joan was standing in her robe. "Oh!" she said, "This is a wonderful wine, and just look at the year."

"I am glad you like it. I will be right back. I am going to take a shower."

As John was taking his shower, he saw through the steam that Joan was watching him. She let her robe fall from her shoulders and joined him in the shower, putting her arms around him and kissing him.

John lifted her gently and stepped out of the shower. He carried her to the bed and lay her there. He climbed in beside her and lifted the covers over them both.

The next day they went all over town looking at things to use in decorating John's house. They went to Sears to find the perfect color of paint, and John saw a huge dog house that would be perfect for Buck. "Look! Buck would love that. Let's get it!"

"Yes," said Joan, "I love all the comforts of home."

That night as they sat in the lounge of their hotel, a trio of Mexican singers was performing, and Joan enjoyed it very much. When the trio took their break, Joan excused herself to the ladies' room to freshen up. John went up to the performers and asked them if they had any other engagements this evening.

When Joan returned, they went up to their room. At nine o'clock they were looking at interior decorating magazines when they heard a beautiful love song being played outside their door. Joan opened it, and there stood the Mexican trio singing the lovely song. Meanwhile, many of the other guests at the hotel also came out of their rooms to see what was happening, and they all enjoyed this romantic move. As the trio finished the song, John handed each man a one-hundred-dollar bill. They departed down the hall singing happily.

"Oh, John, that was lovely!" Joan exclaimed as she put her arms around him.

As the months passed, Joan and John fell truly in love, and there was nothing they would not have done for the other. The house in Maine was taking a little longer with all of Joan's ideas, but it was still going smoothly.

Two weeks before Christmas, they were in Macy's department store, and John turned to Joan and said, Look, the company wants me to go to Japan to show some new layouts, but before I go, I wanted to ask you something . . . ."

Joan looked into his eyes. "Yes, John? Tell me," she said gently.

"How would you like to live with me in my new house as my wife?" he said.

Joan dropped all the packages she had been holding and threw her arms around John's neck. "Yes! Yes!" she said. "There is nothing in the whole world that I would like better than to be you're wife and live with you in that beautiful house!"

Things could not have been better for them over the next few days. On the day of John's departure, he took an early flight and was gone as the sun was rising.

That evening Joan sat alone at home, feeling a little lonely. She heard a knock on the door and went to see who it could be. It was John's boss, Tony. She was surprised to see him but he looked very sad, so she invited him in. Tony told her that John's plane had disappeared about eight hundred miles off the coast of California.

Joan was too shocked to even move at first, but then she started to cry, and she could not stop. "There is still a chance he might be alive. We just cannot know," Tony tried to comfort her.

After Tony left, Joan went upstairs and began to look at her happiest pictures of John. She thought of all they had shared, and she cried herself to sleep.

Tony returned to the office and sat in John's office sadly surveying all of the good work John had done. Soon the sun was rising and Tony was stunned to hear the phone ring.

12

It was the Coast Guard, calling to tell Tony that the plane had been found! It had malfunctioned over the Pacific Ocean, and the pilot maneuvered it along long enough to allow rescue teams to get all the passengers off. No one had been harmed.

Tony was so happy he could hardly believe his ears. He dropped the phone on the desk before the man was finished talking, and rushed to tell Joan. When he got to her door, he had a huge smile on his face. He told her the good news, and she cried tears of pure joy. She threw her arms around Tony in her happiness.

"It's okay now," Tony said.

"Yes," said Joan, "everything is okay."

At the wedding John looked very handsome, and Joan was a beautiful bride, as they stood facing the priest. Then John took Joan's hand and as he placed the ring on her finger, he looked into her eyes with pure love.

Dream Searchers

Far away, in another universe, there was a new world called Dreams. This world was the stuff of dreams! Only a handful of people made it their home. Their powers were as great as people wanted to believe. The sixty people who lived there believed there was a reason that the Creator pulled them there and gave them unbelievable powers.

They traveled to our world to look for people whose dreams were pure and wise. In order to travel to other worlds, these people went just like shooting stars. These people were not violent at all; they were very peaceful, although they were not angels either. They had the power to read people's minds if they are pure and good. When they find such a person, they take them to Dreams, and they make them forget their destination. That is their gift, their legacy.

A woman named Fire, a strong person at heart, was kind of in charge of the world of Dreams. Fire was always looking for dreams throughout the universe. She knew that the dreams are waiting for people like her to pull them out of the pure people. Deep down inside Fire knew that she was somebody else. She had a vision of the most holy lady ever created. As Fire spoke to the others, she told them that they had all been chosen for this destiny and that now they all must go in search of the dreams of the pure.

All sixty people left in search of dreams with goodness, and Fire left for her destination, the planet Earth, rich with dreams to be fulfilled. As the dream searchers left, they appeared in all shades and color, which are caused by the shooting stars.

One dream searcher kept to a world where all they did was dream. As he scanned for dreams, he came to a man of old age with a long white beard and long white hair. After the dream searcher floated above the man for a short while, he turned back into a shooting star and returned to the world of Dreams. The dream searcher knew what the man had dreamt. Since he had been a boy, he had wanted to make music boxes. As the dream searcher put the man into the tank of dreams, the man closed his eyes, and the dreams began.

Back on earth Fire began to scan for pure dreams. She came upon a boy, a small boy. She knew what it was that the boy had always dreamed of. This boy had been abandoned and had always wanted a family. As she floated above him, he turned into a shooting star and left with Fire to the world of Dreams.

At the same time other dream searchers were returning with other pure people, and the old man was living out his dreams. In a house by a great mountain his dreams began. As a man in his twenties, making music boxes that came to life. The first music box went to a clock and every hour as music played, he would come out and chop wood. After a few seconds he would go right back into his log cabin.

The boy's dreams were pure. He was with his father, and they were going down a rough river white-water rafting in the midst of a beautiful landscape. Fire was pleased with these dreams.

The next music box was a woman, and every hour she came out of her cottage and watered her flowers as birds and deer gathered all around her. As the boy continued to dream, he was at home with his mother, his sister, and his father. As they ate dinner, the young boy had a big smile on his face as he looked at his family with joy. A man that one of the dream searchers had brought back with him always dreamed of making clocks, clocks that told the time and the weather with funny faces and eyes that moved. Usually the clocks would make the sound of the animals. As Fire watched, she was impressed with the dreams and visions of the people.

Now the boy was sitting on his father's lap with his sister as his father was telling stories. The boy rested his head on his father's shoulder and was truly happy. Meanwhile, a woman who loved to make dolls began her dream. She was in a house by a brook with colorful landscapes and tall trees all around her. As she made a doll, it would come to life and watch her make another one. The music box maker was making a really nice one. On the hour a man would come out of his house, snow would start to fall, deer would run by, a bear would try to get honey up in a tree, and the man would begin clearing snow from in front of the door as beautiful music filed the air. Meanwhile, the doll maker was making more dolls. The ones that were already made said "hello" to her and asked her to make more dolls to be their friends. As Fire watched, she grew more and more happy.

The boy was having a wonderful time going to town events and picnics as well as playing sports with his father and friends. He was always hugging his father with joy. The music box maker had time to make one more music box before the dream searchers took him back home and made him forget what had happened and where he had been. The last music box he made had a trio coming out of a pair of drums and play music notes that floated into the air.

Fire thought that they were a wonderful set of music boxes. Then the dream searches took him back to where they had found him and left shooting stars for Dreams. Then they took the clock maker back to his world where they had found him, and returned to their own world.

The doll maker had dolls all around her with beautiful dresses and hats to match. They all had green eyes. It was time for her to go home, so the dream searches took her back and then left for the world of Dreams.

Then as Fire watched, the boy sat next to his father with tears in his eyes. "Father, you will never leave me, will you?" he asked.

"No, that will never happen," his father told him.

The boy hugged his father. The boy had a big smile on his face. His mother and sister, who had been listening, were also happy.

Fire had tears falling from her eyes. All of the other dream searchers had gone. Fire just stood there watching. Then suddenly she heard a voice: "Mary, I am pleased with thee. This is good." Then Fire knew who she was. She was the mother of God.

The Lord told her to find a family for the boy. Her instructions were to make him understand that it would always be his family.

"Yes, my Lord."

A short while later they were on Earth, standing in front of a nice little house. As the boy walked up to the door, a man opened the door and said, "Hello, son. How was school?"

"It was okay," he said. Then he said "hello" to his mother and his sister.

"Okay, John, it's time to wash up for dinner," his mother told him.

As Fire watched, she disappeared into the heavens above. As she reached heaven, the Lord said to her, "Mary, this was a very good deed in my eyes. I would like to talk to you about an idea I have."

"Yes, my Lord," she said.

So Mary and the Lord disappeared into the holy clouds.

Dedicated to People Who Search for Their Dreams.

Jill Haywood

Jill Haywood was a very smart woman. She knew a lot about self defense and was a bomb expert. Her father, Tom, was a sergeant in the United States

Army. At a young age Jill's father started teaching her the art of self-defense. He also encouraged her interest in explosives.

Jill's mother passed away when she was younger, and since then Tom devoted much of his attention on their only child. Jill lover her father very much and was always amazed at how he handled his men with honor and courage. She always thought of her father as a man with a big heart. Jill and her father had many things in common, and they spent a lot of time together over the years.

When Jill was twenty-nine years old, her father was ordered to go overseas to the Middle East. Jill was worried about her father because she did not think he would be safe. All she could think about were the many cases of terrorist attacks against the armed forces, but she tried not to worry because she knew that her father was a very careful man and would do his best to stay out of harm's way. She knew she would miss having her father around the house they shared in Pennsylvania. One of the special things about their home was the number of eagles that lived nearby. Jill and her father spent many hours feeding them fish, their favorite food.

A short while after her father had arrived in the Middle East, Jill heard a knock on her door. It was Captain Walker. As he raised his eyes to look at her, she could see that they were filled with sadness. She began to worry, knowing deep down that he had bad news for her. "Jill, I'm afraid I have something to tell you."

"Tell me," she said.

"I'm sorry, but somehow a group of terrorists were able to plant a bomb in a USO building. It exploded during a birthday celebration for one of the men in our platoon."

"Oh my God! My father?!" Jill asked, starting to panic.

"Your father was at the celebration . . . . I'm so sorry, Jill."

Jill burst into tears and ran off into the woods, unable to contain her grief. She looked up to the sky. "Father!" she yelled in anger and sadness. Every eagle in the woods turned its eyes to Jill.

Just them, Jill heard Captain Walker looking for her in the woods. "Jill, where are you?!" he called out.

She didn't answer but waited for him to find her. When he came upon her, she was standing silently with tears in her eyes. "Jill, is there anything I can do?" the captain asked her.

"No, please, I just need to be alone!" she said.

"All right, Jill, but promise me something. If you ever need anything, anything at all, don't hesitate to let me know, okay?"

"Okay. Thank you. I promise."

Then the captain turned and made his way out of the woods to his car. Alone again, Jill was overcome by her grief. She sank to her knees and began to cry helplessly. All of a sudden, Jill looked up with a start. A flash of light caught her attention. She looked around and saw every eagle in the

16

distance—some perched in trees, others upon rocks—struck by a brilliant light. As the eagles were struck by the light, they began to fly from their perches toward her, and within moments the eagles surrounded her.

She had always loved eagles, and she had always thought that they were very intelligent, but to her amazement the eagles began to communicate their thoughts into her mind. She couldn't understand what was happening to her. "What is happening, my friends?" she silently asked.

The eagles told her that they were sorry for the loss of her father and that they would miss him as well.

"How can we be communicating like this?" Jill wondered.

"We do not know either," the eagles said telepathically, in answer to Jill's thoughts, "but maybe something good will come of it."

Just then Jill heard the sound of a car pull up. She recognized the sound of the car. It was Jill's lover, a man named Harrison Cook. He was formerly a Green Beret and currently a science teacher. He had gone to the house looking for Jill and had found the front door wide open. He knew that Jill loved the woods, and so he went to look for her there. He was slightly worried because it was not like Jill to leave the door open.

When Jill emerged from the woods, she ran to him with tears in her eyes. Harrison gave her a hug and then asked, "Jill, what's the matter?"

"Come on, let's go in the house," she said to him through her sobs. When they were inside, Jill pulled herself together and explained what had happened. When she finished, Harrison said, "Why do I have the feeling that there's something you're not telling me?"

"Harrison, I've decided I'm going to the Middle East."

"What?! Jill, that's crazy! Why?" Harrison asked.

"It's something that I have to do."

"Can't you let the military take care of this?" he asked.

"No" She left her seat and started pacing, planning everything in her head. "Your friends, they're ex-Green Berets. Maybe they would help," she said.

Harrison shook his head. When Jill got an idea, it was useless trying to talk her out of it. He went and looked out of the window. He saw many eagles perched on trees in the front yard of Jill's home. "Well, look at that!" he said. "Have you ever seen so many eagles gathered in one place?"

"Those are my friends. They're coming with me to the Middle East," Jill said.

"You must be kidding," Harrison said.

Jill took Harrison's arm. "Come on outside and I'll show you," she said and pulled him by the arm out the front door.

Silently Jill asked all the eagles to gather around her. Harrison was amazed. "Harrison, don't you see? They can help," Jill said. "They can read my thoughts, and I will ask them to find out who is responsible for the bombing. And when they find out, they will tell me."

17

Jill told Harrison the rest of her plan. The eagles were the key. With their strong talons, they could carry bombs and drop them on the enemy. She did not want to use them, but she realized that this was their country, too. They were the American symbol of freedom, and she knew that they would do anything they could to fight for justice for an American soldier. Harrison agreed. Harrison told her that he had a friend who had a great boat they might be able to borrow, and he would contact him right away, as well as his friends from the Green Berets.

"Great!" said Jill. "I will take care of the eagles, and leave the explosives to me," she said with a little smile.

Harrison smiled back. "Good luck," he said as he went to use the telephone. He had a lot of calls to make, and he had to arrange to take a two-week leave from work.

In a quiet room Jill began to wire her explosives. She handled them with patience and the skill of a professional. She made each of them small enough to be carried through the air but concentrated enough to be very deadly.

Harrison contacted his friends, and three of his best buddies agreed to join them. Frank was a weapons' expert, and he was deadly throwing knives. Scott was a real mountain man and could even scale a sheer wall. He also loved sailing, and he was glad to let them borrow his boat. Willie was kind of crazy and liked to have fun, but he was also responsible and courageous when the situation called for it.

They met on the boat later that afternoon and sat around catching up. Harrison told them about Jill and her special connection with the eagles. He told them her psychic powers were developing more all the time and that she could read their minds as well.

The next day, as they were getting the boat ready and loading their equipment onto it, Jill arrived at the pier with a duffel bag hanging from each shoulder and at least ten eagles behind her.

As she got on the boat, all of the eagles began landing on top of the mast. A truck pulled up and Jill called to the guys, "Hey, guys! Can you help me?"

Frank and Willie got out of the truck. "What can we do for you?" Frank asked.

"Can you help me with this?" Jill asked.

"What is it?"

"It's fish for the eagles," she told them.

"Sure we can," said Willie.

They helped Jill get the bags onto the boat and loaded the supplies from the truck as well. By the time they set sail, the sun was just beginning to set. Out at sea the men were checking their weapons. Frank was practicing his knife-throwing skills. He got a bull's eye every time.

Harrison and Jill were below deck checking each bomb. The next afternoon Jill came up on deck and looked up to see the eagles circling the boat.

18

"Look!" Scott said, "It looks like they're communicating with each other!"

"Yes," said Jill. "They are. They're making plans as well."

"Really," said Scott. "That's unbelievable!" He began to climb up the mast.

"Why are you climbing up there?" Jill asked.

"To stay in shape. Why else?" he said.

Willie was getting the ropes ready for Scott as they got close to the coast. When they got to shore, they lowered the anchor and climbed out of the boat to scout around. Silently Jill told the eagles to go do some scouting of their own, so most of them went inland. One eagle stayed with them.

After a while they found an abandoned house, and they waited there for news from the eagles.

"Jill, when this is all over and we go home, would you like to get married?" Harrison asked her.

I've been wondering when you would make your move. I'd love to marry you, Harrison."

Meanwhile, two of the eagles were flying around a mountain when they found a fortress hidden in the mountainside.

They flew close enough to hear the terrorists inside discussing ways to cover up the USO bombing. They heard one of the terrorists say, "Yes, we can thank our friend Major Con for showing us that money is more important than your own country."

The eagles hurried back to the abandoned house that the group was staying in. They silently told Jill everything that they had heard. After a few moments Jill turned to Harrison. "They were betrayed for money, Harrison. I know who they are, and I know where they are." She turned to the others. "Let's get ready," she said to them.

Scott got his lines ready, while the others prepared. "Wait a minute," Harrison said. "Why do we want to climb the mountain when we could just send the eagles in with the bombs to blow everything to hell?"

"No," Jill interrupted. "I want to take care of the head terrorist personally."

"Then what?" asked Harrison.

"Then we blow it to hell," Jill said.

"They packed all of their equipment into a truck. Jill instructed them how to find the mountain fortress.

The arrived at the base of the mountain, got out of the truck and stood at the foot of the mountain. Four of the eagles carried lines in their beaks up the mountainside and wrapped them securely around a tree. Everyone went up except Frank, who stayed below. As they reached the top, they saw a guard standing a few feet ahead. Willie sneaked up behind him and gave him a swift kick, and the guard rolled down the side of the mountain. As they came upon a separate entrance of the fortress, one of the eagles said to Jill, "He's in there."

Jill went through the first door. As the guard who was there reached for his gun, Jill blew him away. The other terrorists heard the gunshot and started coming for Jill. All at once, the eagles attacked, using their beaks and their claws.

Jill heard the sound of water running. She made her way to the next room and saw the leader taking a shower. He tried to get his gun, but Jill told him that if he went for it, she would blow his balls off. He moved away from the gun and put his hands up.

Harrison and Scott walked into the room. "Put your pants on and let's go," Harrison told him.

When they got to where Scott's lines were, Jill turned to the terrorists and said, "Start climbing down, or I'll throw you off!"

The eagles were keeping the men back. After they were down, they went back to the abandoned house, and Jill put the bombs into the eagle's claws.

On top of the mountain, the remaining terrorists were getting ready to get into a helicopter. All ten eagles flew over the fortress in different positions. They released the bombs from their claws and destroyed everything, sending the men and the helicopter down the mountain. One of the eagles flew to where the terrorists' bombs were and released his bomb. The blast leveled half of the mountain.

As the group got back to the boat, they set sail and disappeared over the horizon. A navy warship saw them in the water and pulled alongside them.

"I'll see you at home," Jill said to the eagles. Harrison said the same thing to his friends.

As they got on deck with the sailors, Jill started to tell the captain what had happened and about Major Con. Two weeks later Major Con was being court-martialled for treason, and Jill and Harrison were married. The eagles still lived outside Jill and Harrison's home and kept guard over them.

The Tunnel

Deep down in the tunnels of the Grand Canyon, dinosaurs have been living for generations. Over the years they have come to understand that in order to survive they would have to go above ground.

They were all very friendly, but it seemed their herbivorous habits were becoming a thing of the past. Over the years they grew more and more friendly, and their mental capabilities grew to a point where they could read the human minds. And so they got the idea that they might be able to get a human to help them.

In South Dakota lived a man named Phil Ban. Phil collected everything that he could on dinosaurs—books, dinosaur models, and broken bits of fossils he had found. Ever since he had been a boy, Phil had believed that dinosaurs had been friendly and must have tried to survive the way that man had.

Phil owned a store where he sold all kinds of things pertaining to dinosaurs. One day a couple of kids came into Phil's store. "Can I help you?" Phil asked them.

"Just looking, sir," the kids said.

Phil went back to stacking some books when he suddenly got a terrible headache. He decided it was nothing and went on with his work, but when he got home after work and was eating dinner, he felt it again. Phil went upstairs to lie down, wondering why he was getting these headaches. As he went to sleep, a pentaceratops began drawing a map of where the dinosaurs were.

After days of this Phil decided to pack some of his things and go to the Grand Canyon. He took his pickup truck, stopping only to fill up with gas and stock up on a lot of goodies. When he finally got to the Grand Canyon, he searched until he saw a familiar path leading down through the craggy stone. He began to descend into the canyon, and as he neared the canyon floor, he said, "I'm here, I'm here."

All of a sudden rocks began to fall as if something was trying to get out. Then it happened: Seven prehistoric animals came out—a pentaceratops, a struthiomimus, a poebrotherium, a pliohippus, a mammuthus, an epigaulus, and a pteranodon, which flew over Phil and landed behind him. Phil stood there in amazement.

All of the dinosaurs gathered around him, and the pentaceratops began communicating with Phil through its mind. "We were always here," it told him. "We need to come to the top. Food is becoming a thing of the past here below. We need land rich with trees and shrubs and foliage."

Phil told them that he understood but that their existence would be a shock of mankind.

"Come into the tunnel with us," they urged him. After walking about a half a mile, Phil saw all of the dinosaur families. There were about six or seven in each.

A baby pliohippus came over to Phil and started to rub its head on Phil's leg. "Just like a cat," Phil said in amazement.

"Oh, yes. He's very charming," the baby's father told Phil.

"But how will I make them believe?" Phil asked them.

"I trust you to take my son with you to the people," a mammuthus father told Phil. A struthiomimus told him that he could take his daughter with him too, it would help.

As the other dinosaurs watched, Phil left with the two young dinosaurs. He left for the governor's mansion with the two babies in the back of his

21

pickup. On the way there, Phil fed them cupcakes, and they really loved them.

When they got to the mansion, the guard could not believe his eyes. He called for the governor to come out.

"Oh my Lord!" the governor said when he saw the dinosaurs. "Where did you find them?"

Phil began to tell the story, and soon everybody was running around like a bunch of chickens with their heads cut off. Everybody was on the telephone with somebody, and the governor called the president. Within four hours, the mansion was filled with curious visitors. The kids were having a ball with baby dinosaurs.

A woman walked up to Phil. "Hi, I'm Mary," she said.

"Yes," said Phil. "You're the president's daughter."

Later Phil was telling the story of what happened to the president, and the president insisted that Phil take him to the tunnels. When they arrived at the tunnels, there were reporters all over the place.

"Would you like to come with me into the tunnels?" Phil asked Mary.

"Yes," she replied.

Phil, Mary, and the two baby dinosaurs went down into the tunnels, and about two hours later, the anxious reporters could hear them returning. First came the family of the pteranodon, flying out over the growing crowd landing right behind them.

The president was shocked. He dropped his cellular telephone and watched in awe as the rest of the dinosaurs emerged from the tunnels. Soon all of the dinosaurs stood around the people.

"Here is what I want," said the president. "I want eighty square miles of land in Florida. I want a wall built around it with just one opening. Get me a general! I want you to get in touch with all of the building companies. I want somebody by all the phones. Let's go, people!"

The president walked over to Phil. "This is something!" he said.

"Mr. President, how are we going to get all of the dinosaurs to Florida?" Phil asked him.

"A wagon train, my boy! A wagon train of dinosaurs!"

Meanwhile, the rest of the world was just receiving the pictures. People at home could not believe what they were seeing on television. The airports, bus stations, train stations, and sea ports were never so busy. People were coming from everywhere!

Back at the Grand Canyon, the president turned to Phil. "Phil, you lead the train. It will take at least a couple of months to get to Florida."

"Would you like to come with me, Mary?" Phil asked the president's daughter.

"You got it!" Mary said to him.

Phil and Mary each took one of the baby dinosaurs with them and started out. The pteranodons left first, since they could fly, and then the train left, guarded by the military.

All around the dinosaurs were news helicopters to photograph and report the progress in addition to military helicopters to guard the strange procession. As they passed through each town, people fed them fruit and nuts and gave water to drink.

"You have done a good thing. You must be a good man if the dinosaurs trust you," Mary said to Phil.

"I guess I've always studied about dinosaurs, and sometimes I have wished that I could have lived in that era, but now *this* is that era."

Mary was feeding the baby dinosaurs bananas, apples, and oranges. The babies were trying to lick Mary and, and she kept giggling.

Meanwhile, the president continued his flurry of phone calls.

"Mr. President, the walls are being built around the clock." his general told him.

"That's good. Have you gotten a hold of the fruit companies yet?"

"Yes sir. Everybody is doing his part."

As the train went through the Lone Star state, the dinosaurs got a welcome that was a sight to behold. Phil told everybody that they could camp there for the night. Everybody had a ball that night playing with the dinosaurs. That night Phil asked Mary if she had a boyfriend.

"No," said Mary, "I was hoping you would ask me out on a date."

Phil looked at one of the dinosaurs. "Well what do you think?" he asked it.

"Go for it," the dinosaur told him.

As the train of dinosaurs continued to move through towns, the people gave them warm greetings. Later the fathers of the dinosaurs went to Phil and Mary. "We will never forget what you have done for us."

"There will be no reason for you to forget. I will be with you for as long as I live," Phil replied. Some of the dinosaurs had tears in their eyes. Mary told Phil she could sense the dinosaurs' hearts were pure.

In Florida the walls were nearly finished. The president was there waiting for the train. He stood in front of the opening.

All of a sudden a Pteranodon came flying over the wall.

"Here they come!" someone yelled.

The president turned to his aide. "I've never seen so many cameras in one place before," he said.

"Yes sir. There are a lot of people who want pictures of this," said his aide.

Phil and Mary followed the dinosaurs into the dinosaurs' new home. Phil looked over and saw a gift shop being built. The president turned to Phil and said, "I want you to run it. The money we make there will pay for the dinosaurs' food and for the upkeep of the grounds."

"I hope you keep your word," Phil said to Mary.

"What do you mean?" Mary asked.

"Well, I hope you will help."

Mary looked into Phil's eyes. "Yes. I will help you for the rest of our lives," she said to him.

Phil took Mary's hand, and they smiled as they watched the dinosaurs enjoying their new home.

Witches

In 1789, in Boston, Massachusetts there were two separate covens of witches—the good ones and the bad ones.

The bad ones were very ugly, with pitch black hair and fingernails. Their nails were their tools for destruction. The bad witches had mastered the power of flight.

The good witches were ordinary, clean-cut people who blended in with everybody else, but they also had strong powers and had mastered the power of flight. They had white nails, which held their powers.

Rachel Scott was the witch that kept order among the good coven, and Tanya Wills was the leader of the bad coven. Rachel knew that Tanya planned to destroy Boston and needed to devise a plan to stop her.

About a mile outside of Salem in an eerie barn, Tanya and her followers gathered together to hold a black mass. As they surrounded an eighteen-year-old girl, Tanya began to hold a black mass. The girl had been brainwashed into becoming the evil witches sacrifice.

Outside, a man named David was passing by when he heard a noise coming from the barn. He found a crack in the sideboards and peeked through. What he saw inside could have only been described as unholy. He looked around and found a good-sized chunk of wood. He kicked the barn door down and stormed inside. Two of the witches came at him. He hit one of them in the face with the piece of wood, and he threw the other one through the barn door. He grabbed the girl away from the other witches and disappeared with her before they could stop him. When they got to safety, David took off his coat and wrapped it around the girl. "What is your name?" he asked her.

"Eve," she told him.

"What was going on back there, Eve?" David asked.

"I don't know," she said to him. "They came at night and forced me into the barn. They said they were going to sacrifice me to . . . the devil."

"Devil worshipers!" David said, barely able to believe it. "Witches to do the devil's evil bidding."

Back at the barn, five evil witches came flying out, heading for town. David saw them, so he took Eve to his barn. "Stay here. You'll be safe," he told her.

"Thank you, David," Eve said, "for saving my life."

"Just stay here," David told her.

David went to get his favorite horse, Monday, from the stables. He rode into town as quickly as he could.

Meanwhile Rachel had a vision and saw all that had happened at the barn and sent four of her witches to scout around town.

As the five evil witches got into town, they used their nails to shoot fire and destroy everything that was in their way.

Rachel's witches were ready, waiting in different parts of town. They started using their powers, shooting fire at the evil ones and watching them drop to the ground and burn.

As David came riding into town, one of the bad witches shot fire at him, but she missed her mark and hit the tavern behind him. David looked down and saw a pitchfork. He grabbed it and stabbed the witch and threw her into the fire.

As David looked up, he saw the good witches flying away. He followed them to a barn. When he got to the barn door, Rachel opened it and said, "Come in, David. I've been waiting for you."

"I've seen something unholy go into your barn." Dave told Rachel.

"There is nothing unholy here, David."

"But I've seen witches come into here."

"They are good witches, not like the ones that you have encountered earlier this evening," Rachel explained. "Please come in and sit. I need to talk to you."

David went inside and sat down as Rachel tried to explain the rest. "Those other witches that you saw, they are the work of Satan. They do Satan's bidding."

"Is there anyway to stop them?" David asked.

"Yes," Rachel said. "There is a way. But first you must go back and get Eve and bring her here because they will come for her again."

So David rode back to his farm on Monday.

Meanwhile, Tanya confronted Satan. Satan told her to get the girl and to burn down David's house. "I will take care of him," Satan told Tanya. So Tanya sent out her witches.

Back at David's barn, Eve saw the witches coming over the trees and ran into the woods and hid. As the bad witches came, they crashed right through the house searching for Eve. "Search everywhere. If we don't bring her back, Tanya won't like it," said one of the witches.

"She's not here," said another. "Let's try the town."

As they left, one of the witches used her nails to set David's house on fire. As David rode up, he saw the house burning and panicked. He ran around, calling out frantically for Eve. Eve came up behind him and tapped his shoulder. Startled, David spun around. "I'm so glad you're alive!" he said as he put his hands on her shoulders. "Now come with me."

They got onto Monday, with Eve riding behind David and resting her head on his back. When they got to Rachel's house David helped her off the horse. He held her and pressed his lips against hers. Rachel was looking out at them and smiled. When they got into the house, Rachel asked, "Are you hungry, Eve?"

"Yes, I could eat a little," Eve told her.

After they had eaten, Rachel turned to David. "Now, David, this spell book I have is basically a book of Satan. There is a way that you might be able to confront Satan on our own terms. You would have to hold this cross in front of him and say, `Let no man be a man without honor.' This will make him fight as a human, without his powers."

"But how will I find him?" David asked her.

"There is a way," Rachel told him. "I will show you where to enter his grounds. If you could beat him, he would withdraw." She paused to think. "Now I have to gather all of my witches to do battle with Tanya and her followers. I will leave two witches here with Eve. David, you come with me."

Meanwhile, Tanya was getting ready to make her move. She sent five of her witches to Rachel's house to get Eve and told the rest to stand by.

As they got to Rachel's house, they attacked from all directions. They used their powers and destroyed the two good witches, but not before they lost three of their own. They got ahold of Eve and left with her, just as Rachel's house went up in smoke. The two remaining evil witches headed for Satan himself as Eve struggled to get free.

As the mist rolled in, Rachel took David to the entrance of Satan's domain. "Good luck, David. Watch your back," Rachel said to him as they took off into the eerie night mist to confront Tanya and her evil witches.

David walked slowly into the cave. As he got deeper into the cave, there were skeletons and skulls all over. *What an eerie sight,* thought David to himself.

Satan, in his lair with Eve, told her to call out David's name or he would rip her heart out. Reluctantly she called out to him, and when he heard her voice, he tightened his fists in anger.

Back in town the people saw two small armies of witches in the sky above them. One army was dressed in black, and the other was clothed in white.

"It's been a long time, Tanya. Let's finish what we started years ago," Rachel said to Tanya. The witches began going at it, with fire spewing from their nails. Good and bad witches were dropping as the people watched in shock. As they fell, they landed in ponds, on houses, or in trees, sometimes setting other things on fire. Rachel and Tanya dodged the shots of fire and preparing to battle each other head-to-head.

Meanwhile, David entered Satan's chamber and saw two witches holding Eve. To his left he saw Satan. He held out the cross and said, "Let no man be a man without honor!"

"Rachel has taught you well," Satan said. "I should have known of this. If you win, she goes free and I will be gone." As Satan stood up, David barreled into him and knocked him over his chair.

"That's good, boy. Now try this," Satan said as he hit David and sent him flying five feet backward. David went at him again, but Satan slapped him, and he went flying again. "How was that, boy? After I finish you, I will make love to Eve and then sacrifice her."

David got up and gave Satan a good punch in the stomach. As he was bent over, Dave hit him in the chin with his knee. Then he got him in a head lock. Satan could not get him off. David kept smashing his face with his fist.

Back in town the battle was almost over. The good witches had won. As Rachel cornered Tanya, Tanya tried to escape, but all of the other good witches used their nails and set her on fire, and she dived into a wooden bridge.

Back in Satan's lair David saw blood running from Satan's mouth and nose. Satan looked at David and said, "Okay, boy, you win. Take her, but never cross my path again."

Eve ran up to David and clung to him.

The next day was beautiful. The townspeople gathered around David, Eve, and Rachel. One man stepped up and said, "I speak for the whole town. You have saved us from an unholy act of sorcery. For this all of the people in our town want to rebuild your houses for you."

Eve turned to David with a big smile. "Would you like to live with me as my wife?" David asked Eve.

"Oh, yes!" Eve said happily and hugged him again.

Meanwhile, Satan sat in his kingdom as red as a ripe apple.

Dedicated to all good witches in the world.

Heart of Gold

Loretta Grant had a very good life. Her grandfather had been a shipbuilder and had built ships for the navy during the war. Her father, Sam, took over the business after her grandfather passed away. He never remarried after his wife, Beth, died in childbirth. It was known in the business world that Sam was worth nine billion dollars in stocks and real estate. Sam devoted much time to Loretta. He used to call her "Spring" because she was like a beautiful spring day.

One day when she fourteen years old, she came home from school and said, "Dad, I'm home."

"Hey, Spring!" Sam said to her.

"Listen, Dad. The girls at school want to farm a softball team, and I told them that I would take care of the uniforms and gloves and anything else we need to play ball," she said.

"I always knew you had a heart of gold," her dad said.

Loretta gave her father a big kiss, and then said, "Dad, I know you must get lonely in this big house. Why don't you go on a date?"

"No, no. I am fine."

"Okay, Dad," Loretta said with a sadness in her eyes.

The next day, Loretta and her friends stopped by a sporting goods shop after school. Afterward they went to the park. They all were having fun, but Loretta noticed about thirty children in the stands wearing torn and dirty clothes. She walked over to the children and said, "Hello." Then she asked the man who was with them what was going on. He told her that the children were from a home for children who had been abandoned or whose parents had died.

That's a real shame," she said as her eyes began to redden. Then she asked if the state took care of them.

"Not a lot," the man told her.

"give me the address of the home," Loretta said to him.

Loretta told her girlfriends about the children she had seen, and they were filled with such compassion that they went to the store and bought video games, televisions, stereo systems, and clothing for them. When Loretta got to the home with all of the gifts, she could hardly believe what she saw. The bedrooms were shameful, and the rest of the house was the same.

The man who took care of the children called them so that they could see what Loretta had brought them. "This girl bought you all of this stuff," he told them. They all began to hug Loretta, and tears came to her eyes.

Six years later Loretta's father passed away. The doctors said that he had died from a broken heart.

One day Loretta was at home watching *Boy's Town*, and she noticed Father Flanagan cutting corners to get money to build the home. She sat back and thought about the children's home and how she could help.

She began to talk to herself. *It is not enough! Something else can be done.* She envisioned all of the children who had never really had anything, not even love.

Loretta got on the telephone to Max Lennon, a great man and her father's closest friend. "Max, this is Loretta. Can I come and see you?"

"Hi, Loretta. Of course you can come see me!"

"Okay, I'll be there in one hour."

When she arrived at Max's home, she explained to him what her plans were. "Max," she said, "you've built some beautiful ships. You've built many other things with my father. I want you to build a children's home in every state."

"Is that what your heart is telling you?" Max asked, turning to Loretta.

"Yes, Max."

"Okay, then. I'll get on it right now," he told her.

"How long do you think it will take?" Loretta asked him.

"About seven years," he told her after some figuring.

"That's good, Max," she said to him.

Later on Max went over to Loretta's house with the finished plan. "Okay, Loretta, here it is. Number one, the whole project will take around seven years to complete. Each home will be up-to-date. The kids will have rooms for themselves, a gym, a movie theatre, and a good-sized kitchen," Max explained to her. "Each one will be built near good schools, and each one will have its own sports field. The entire cost will be somewhere around three-and-a-half billion dollars."

"That is no problem," Loretta said. "I still have at least five billion."

Two years passed by, and Loretta was at the opening of every children's home. Loretta liked to visit the homes when they were finished and see how they had turned out. They built one home for boys and one for girls, and as soon as they were finished, the children moved in. They got new clothing, and they were very happy. Loretta made sure that the homes had good people running them.

After a while Max noticed that Loretta wasn't doing much of anything unless it had to do with children's homes. "Loretta, you have to get out and enjoy yourself! Go find a man. This isn't good."

Turning to Max, Loretta said, "I will, Max. I will."

Two-and-a-half years later, sixty percent of the homes were finished. Loretta was twenty-five years old and her face was on the cover of every newspaper and magazine. It seemed like the whole world was watching what she was doing. To the people her heart was the purest of gold.

Loretta spent most of her time visiting the children. She was always talking with them. They loved her, and that was the bottom line. She loved them, too, no matter what race or religion they were. In Loretta's eyes they were the future. Kids from the homes were always sending her letters and cards.

When the last of the homes was built, Loretta looked at Max and said, "Thank you, Max. Thank you."

When she got home, she went into the room of her house where she kept all the cards and letters she got from the children, and tears came to her eyes. She looked at a picture of her mother and said, "I did it, Mom. I made my dream come true."

When she was twenty-seven, she went to see her lawyer, Tom Miller so she could have a will drawn up. She wanted all of the money set up in a fund for the children's homes, so that it would always be there for the keepers of the homes.

Tom looked at Loretta. "Are you all right?" he asked her.

"Yes," she said.

"Loretta, I've known you since you were a child. Are you sure everything is okay?" he asked again.

"Yes, I'm fine, Tom."

Three years later Loretta suddenly checked herself into a hospital. Max came to visit her immediately. "Loretta, what's wrong?" he asked her.

"Oh, Max, I'm just feeling a little weak. I'm all right," she assured him.

"Are you sure?"

"Yes, I'm all right."

"Okay, I'll be right back," Max told her as he left to find the doctor.

"Hey, doc," he said when he saw him, "what's wrong with Loretta?"

"I'm sorry to tell you this, but she might have what her father had," the doctor told him.

"A broken heart," Max said quietly. Then he looked at the doctor. "Why?" he asked him.

The doctor could only shake his head. After a couple of weeks had passed, Loretta was still in the hospital. Many of the children from the homes she had built came to see her. Max did a good job keeping the news reporters away.

One day Loretta turned to Max and said, "Max, will you take care of the homes for me?"

"Yes," Max said as he began to cry. "Loretta, don't do this!" he sobbed.

Loretta put her head back to rest and looked up. "Mother," she said, and her eyes closed for ever.

At the cemetery it was sight to behold. There were more flowers in one place than anybody had ever seen, and all kinds of people were paying their respects. Max watched mutely, silently asking, *Why, Lord? Tell me why.*

The children from the homes lined up as far as the eye could see. Throughout the world tears were shed, and for Loretta the bells would toll.

After three months the president called a special meeting in Congress and on national television. "Loretta Grant will live in many children's hearts and for many many years," the president said to people throughout the world. "This woman truly had a heart of gold." The president took out his handkerchief. "I do not know why she was taken. The Lord must want her at his side." He paused to wipe his eyes. "How do you honor someone like Loretta Grant? This medal which I am holding is given to brave people—not just to people who have fought in wars, because there are other kinds of battles. So, we, the people of America, present this medal of honor to a woman with a heart of gold!"

Dedicated to anyone who has a heart of gold.

Supermarket

In Houston, Texas Scott Hayward was getting ready for work. He worked for a supermarket and had been there for twenty years. He started work after the store closed. He cleaned up and restocked the groceries. He always got to work early so that he could have a cup of coffee and some donuts.

"Hi, Scott. Early again?" asked one of his co-workers. "How was your day?"

"Oh, the same as usual. Nothing ever changes," Scott answered. He sat in the back of the store finishing his coffee and donuts and then took a nap. Hew woke up about twenty minutes before his shift. The other workers were leaving for the night so Scott made sure that the doors were locked and the alarm was set before he got to work.

As he was sweeping the cereal aisle, he heard giggling coming from the other side of the store. "All right, who's over there?" he said loudly. "Is somebody playing games?" He walked over to the side of the store where they sold men's underclothes, which is where the noise had been coming from. Then just as he got there, he heard noises coming from the cereal aisle. When he got back over there, he saw that there was cereal all over the floor. Scott stared at the mess in confusion. He knew he had just swept. All of a sudden, he heard somebody say, "Ho, ho, ho, Green Giant."

"All right, now I know somebody is in here!" Scott said. He was starting to get a little annoyed.

Then from the men's department he heard someone say that he was not wearing Fruit of the Looms. Then the giggling started again.

Scott went around the store checking to make sure all of the doors were locked. They all were.

Scott told himself that he must be hallucinating from all of the donuts he had eaten earlier. Back in the cereal aisle arms were coming out of cereal boxes, and they were throwing cereal at each other. Scott could hear what was going on and ran over. He jumped in front of the aisle, but nobody was there. What he did see, however, was a mess of cereal all over the floor. Scott didn't know what was going on. Again he heard someone say, "Ho, ho, ho, Green Giant."

In a panic he asked himself if he was losing his mind. As the giggling started again, Scott said, "All right, whoever you are, you had better come out, or I'll call the police!" But the giggling kept getting louder.

All of a sudden Mr. Clean came out of his bottle and stretched his arms. "It feels good to be out of there," he said.

Scott couldn't believe his eyes. *Was this really Mr. Clean?* he wondered.

"We have been watching you work in this supermarket for twenty years, Scott, and we feel that today it is time to have some fun!" said Mr. Clean.

"I haven't had any fun in years," Scott said.

So with Mr. Clean leading the way, they returned to the cereal aisle, and Mr. Clean told everybody to come on out. As they all came out of their boxes, Scott put his hands on his head in amazement. He watched as Tony the Tiger; Captain Crunch; Snap, Crackle, and Pop; the Trix Rabbit; the Sugar Bear; and Toucan Sam came out of their boxes. And from the canned vegetables came the Jolly Green Giant.

Mr. Clean got on top of some soda cases and blew his whistle. He had a microphone in his hand called for everyone's attention.

"Wait a minute!" said Scott. "Where are the guys with the giggles?"

"Here we are, Scott!" said the Fruit of the Loom guys as they pulled on his pants and giggled some more.

"All right, boys," said Mr. clean, "stand over there and be quiet." Mr. Clean told everybody that it was time to have a war. The cereal guys got their slingshots and catapults. The Green Giant got his pea shooter, and the Fruit of the Loom guys stood back to watch. Mr. Clean asked Scott what he was going to use. Scott picked marshmallows and a slingshot.

"Let it begin!" Mr. Clean said over his microphone.

Scott got behind the toilet paper with his marshmallows. Captain Crunch tolled out with his big cannon on his hip. Toucan Sam wasted no time in dropping cereal on the Rice Krispies guys. The Green Giant was shooting at Scott with peas, so Scott started shooting marshmallows with his slingshot.

"Here it is!" said Mr. Clean with his microphone. Captain Crunch was bombing Snap, Crackle, and Pop. The Trix Rabbit was going after the Sugar Bear. "Look at that! Scott just got the Jolly Green Giant in the mouth! I tell you I've never seen anything like this! Here comes Scott running and shooting at the Sugar Bear at the same time!"

Now the Rice Krispies guys were doing really well. They even made the Trix Rabbit go back inside his box. Captain Crunch was blowing Tony the Tiger away with his cannon. Scott started running after the Rice Krispies guys and shot them from behind. The Green Giant got behind Scott and started to hit him. Toucan Sam started to bomb the Jolly Green Giant. The Trix Rabbit came back out and started to get the Sugar Bear. Meanwhile Tony the Tiger was getting Snap, Crackle, and Pop with his slingshot. All of a sudden the Fruit of the Loom guys walked up, holding a stick with a white flag on it.

"We have a truce!" Mr. Clean said.

Scott looked closely at the flag and said, "Those are my shorts they have on that stick!" Mr. Clean told Scott that was because he was not wearing Fruit of the Looms. "I'm going to get you guys!" Scott told them.

So, the Fruit of the Loom guys bent over, put their butts together, and started to bang them together. In the background the theme song from "My Three Sons" came on. Meanwhile the Rice Krispie guys were hitting everything with their cereal. A lot of cereal was hitting Aunt Jemima's syrup bottle. She came out with a broom and went after them. "I'll teach you guys to throw cereal at my bottle!" she told them.

Tony the Tiger was doing pretty well at holding his ground. "Can I stay with you?" the Sugar Bear asked Tony.

"Sure," Tony said, "got your slingshot?"

"Right here!" said Sugar Bear.

Scott got behind the Fruit of the Loom guys and started bombing them with his marshmallows. The Trix Rabbit was pummeling Captain Crunch; three times he got cereal in the captain's mouth. The Jolly Green Giant was getting Toucan Sam pretty good. Toucan Sam dove right back into his box. Mr. Clean told everybody that they had lost Toucan Sam.

Captain Crunch turned on the Trix Rabbit, so the rabbit jumped back into his box also. Scott got on top of the toilet paper and let the Jolly Green Giant have it with his marshmallow. The giant went back into his box also. Scott got on top of the toilet paper and let the Jolly Green Giant have it with his marshmallows. The giant went back into his can. The battle was over. Mr. Clean blew the final whistle.

Scott walked over to Mr. Clean and said, "That was great! I have never had so much fun."

Mr. Clean looked out and saw that the sun was getting ready to rise. Everybody came out of their boxes to say good-bye to Scott—even the Fruit of the Loom guys. "Maybe we can do it again sometime," Mr. Clean said.

So there Scott stood, looking down at the huge mess.

Well, he said to himself, *it's time to go to work.*

The next thing he knew he was being awakened. "Are you all right?" a co-worker asked him.

"Yes, yes," Scott said. "I must have been dreaming." Scott locked up the store and checked all the alarms again. He got to the cereal aisle and began to clean up. All of a sudden he heard giggling and then he heard someone say, "Ho, ho, ho, Green Giant."

Harmony

Astronaut Bill Wright got his stuff together. He was getting ready for the mission he was scheduled to go on early the next morning.

Bill's will had passed away three weeks ago, and he had an eight-year-old son.

"I want you to be a good boy for Aunt Betty, okay?" Bill said to his son, Jeff.

"Okay, Dad. I'll be good," Jeff said.

When they got to the space center, Bill picked up his son and gave him a big kiss on his cheek. As he left, he watched his son waving good-bye.

In the shuttle with the other astronauts, Bill got ready for lift-off. The other astronauts slapped Bill on the back and told him they were sorry about his wife.

The countdown began, and as the shuttle departed, Bill's son watched it disappear into the sky.

On their second day in space, Bill and another astronaut, Ted, were scheduled to do some work outside the ship. As they were doing their repairs, Bill's line broke, and he went floating off into space. Ted was powerless. There was nothing he could do except watch helplessly as Bill disappeared into the darkness of outer space. As Bill floated, you could see in his eyes the vision of happy times with his wife and son.

The men in the shuttle just looked at each other with tears in their eyes. "What about his boy? Who's going to tell him?" they asked each other.

Bill could see from his meter that his air supply would only last about another half an hour. He closed his eyes and wondered what was going to happen to his son. All of a sudden he saw an object heading towards him. It pulled up right next to him. It was round, bright blue in color, and had a row of windows going around it. Suddenly a ramp came out, and two people took Bill aboard. Then they left at the speed of light.

By this time, bill had passed out, so the men hooked earphones on Bill to see what was going through his mind. The men, Lance and Mack, looked at each other and shook their heads when they saw what was going on in Bill's mind.

"Relax, Bill," said Lance as Bill began to wake up.

"How did you know my name?" bill asked him.

"We have ways. We will tell you about that, but not right now," he told him. Then he said, "You are all right. You are safe."

Bill started to look around. "I've never seen anything like this before," Bill said.

"Yes, we know," said Mack. "Just relax. We're traveling at the speed of light."

As they entered their world, Bill looked out the window. He saw three suns and skies so blue that it looked unreal. He looked down and saw trains with no tracks and buildings that looked like bubbles. Some were bigger than any building on Earth. When they landed, Mack and Lance took Bill to the president of their world. "That was some ride you had there," the president said to Bill. "You were lucky Mack and Lance were out there." Then he asked for a woman named Tanya to come into the room. She said Hello to Bill, and the president told her that he wanted her to show Bill around the city and explain to him how things worked there.

As they walked out, Bill noticed that there were elevators about one-hundred-feet tall taking people up to ramps to get on trains. He also noticed the cars that flew in a special lane with bright colors. Each car had the last name of the family who owned it printed on the side. On the street he looked at all kinds of stores. Tanya explained to Bill that the president took care of everybody's wants and needs–health care, homes, vacations, everything. The people never were in need.

"It would be so good if Earth was like this," Bill said to Tanya. "Earth will be like this in about eight hundred years," Tanya told him. She looked at him more closely. "You seem kind of sad," she said.

"Yes," Bill said. "My boy back on earth is only eight-years-old, and my wife died three weeks ago."

"Yes, I know. Mack and Lance told me," she said. "In two days we will be taking you back to Earth. You have a choice, Bill. You can return here with your little boy, or you can stay on Earth. You have two days to decide."

As they finished looking around the city, Bill was amazed at the pets he saw with people. Some had tigers, and others had lions. He even saw one couple with an alligator as a pet.

"They are all gentle," Tanya said to Bill when she saw the look of amazement on his face. "Nobody eats meat like they do on earth. That was outlawed eight hundred years ago."

"That's a really good thing," Bill said.

"It takes time to get harmony," Tanya said to him.

So Tanya took Bill to where the people did their food shopping. There were miles and miles of fruit and nut trees. There were vegetable gardens and fields of grain. Bill turned to Tanya with a smile. "My son loves fruit and nuts," Bill said as he looked at her. He was looking at her in a different way than he had before.

They got to Tanya's car, and Bill said, "Wow! This is some car. It's shaped like a pyramid!"

"Yes," said Tanya smiling. "Now we are going to the ocean."

When they got there, Bill could not believe his eyes. He saw children water-skiing with dolphins pulling them along. Whales were giving children rides on their backs. What fun even the whales and dolphins were having! "I can not believe this!" Bill said to her.

"The children here love school," Tanya added. When school is out, they enjoy going to camps."

"That's really great!" said Bill.

"Are you hungry?" Tanya asked.

"Yes," said Bill. "I am very hungry."

Tanya took Bill to where he would be staying and told him that she would be back in an hour. Bill sat in a chair in the house and waited. He thought of all the things he had seen, and he wondered what Jeff would think of all this.

After a while, Bill heard a knock at the door. It was Tanya, and she was looking real fine to Bill's eyes. As they ate dinner, Bill watched in fascination as the sun set behind the mountains. What a beautiful sight! The colors were just like a rainbow.

Tanya looked at Bill and said, "I would love to see you and your son come back here, Bill."

"Yes," agreed Bill, with his eyes sparkling. "Me too."

"I am going back to earth with you, Mack, and Lance. I really want to meet your boy," Tanya said, looking at Bill.

They smiled at each other.

The day for departure had come. With the president standing by, they took off at the speed of light. Bill got a smile on his face. "Can you get to Earth without them knowing?" he asked.

Mack smiles. "No problem," he said.

They entered the Earth's atmosphere and landed the spaceship just outside Bill's sister's house. Bill knocked on the door and Betty opened it.

"Bill!" she exclaimed, giving him a hug. "I can't believe it!"

Bill's son runs into the room. "Dad," he said with tears in his eyes. Everyone's eyes filled with tears. Bill said, "I want you to meet Tanya."

Tanya stepped forward. "Jeff," she said, "I have heard a lot about you." Jeff was amazed by all of the interesting things about the planet, and he asked Tanya to tell him more about it. Tanya gladly told him about the children on her planet. She told him about summer camp and the cars and many other things.

Bill then introduces everyone else to each other. Lance, Mack," he said, "this is my sister Betty.

Lance stepped forward. "Pleased to meet you," he said with his eyes sparkling.

"Very nice to meet you," Betty said, returning his smile. Bill talked his sister into going back with them.

They all got on the ship. Betty sat next to Lance, and he got a smile bigger than Bill's was. They took off to the new world at the speed of light. As they approached the planet, Jeff looked down and said, "Dad, there are no train tracks!"

"Come here, Jeff," Tanya said. Jeff came over and sat next to her. As they look out the window, they all witness the setting of the three suns, just minutes apart.

Bill turned to Tanya. "You know, I don't know the name of the planet."

Tanya took Bill's hand in hers. "It's Harmony, Bill."

The Ghost of Laurel and Hardy

Joe Marsh was always trying to be a funny guy. All through his school years, he loved the slapstick comedy of Laurel and Hardy. He was always writing stories about slapstick and sending them to Hollywood, hoping for an answer. Hollywood seemed to think that slapstick was a thing of the past, but Joe kept trying with his stories. At dinner Joe's mother encouraged him not to give up his dream because it was time for Hollywood to change a little and do something for the laughter of the people. He couldn't sit around and wait any longer. He had to get his life together. He went upstairs to think. He laid on his bed, closed his eyes, and began to dream. All of a sudden Joe heard noises coming from the floor, so he got up and put his head to the floor. As he was sitting there, out popped Stan Laurel and Oliver Hardy. As Stan tried to get out, he got stuck between the floor boards and started crying and scratching his head.

"Would you stop fooling around?" Oliver asked him, annoyed.

"I'm not fooling around, "I'm stuck!" Stan replied, still crying.

"You can't do anything right!" Oliver said.

Joe went to help him and got a fist planted in his eye. Finally Stan got free.

"What happened? I'm seeing two of you!" Joe asked.

"You'll be all right in a minute," Oliver told him.

Then Oliver said "hello" to Joe because he had not done so yet.

"That goes for me, too," added Stan.

"Let me do the talking!" Oliver said as he turned to Stan.

Stan started to cry. "I want to talk too!"

"Now, now." Oliver wagged his finger at Stan. "This is a fine mess we're in."

"What are you guys doing here? You're dead," Joe asked them.

Oliver told Joe that they were going to take him back to 1929, when slapstick was king. "We are going to show you the true meaning of slapstick," Oliver told him.

"that's right, just like he said," Stan said.

Oliver turned to Stan. "Can't you shut up for a minute?"

"I want to help too!" Stan said as he started to cry again.

"You know, you two guys have mad a lot of people laugh over the years, and it still goes on now, but the younger generation needs to get a taste of the true slapstick," Joe said to them both.

"That's right!" Stan said.

"What do you mean 'that's right'?" Oliver asked, turning to Stan. Oliver lifted up his arm and shook his head. Then they turned to Joe and asked if he was ready.

"Yes, I'm ready," Joe answered. So Oliver took him through the floor, and the landed in 1929. Stan came after him but didn't make it all the way through. All they could see were his legs. Joe and Oliver tried to get ahold of his legs, but Stan kicked both of them in the eyes. Finally Stan dropped to the ground and looked at their black eyes. Joe kicked Stan in the seat, so Stan picked up a brick and threw it at them, accidentally breaking a window.

The people of 1929 saw Laurel and Hardy as real people, of course, not as ghosts. So the man whose window got broken came out and asked who had thrown the brick. Stan pointed at Oliver.

"What do you mean I broke the window?" Oliver asked.

"You see?" said Stan. "He just said that he broke the window!"

So the man picked up the brick and hit Oliver over the head with it. The whole time Joe just watched, laughing.

Oliver picked up a brick, pointed to the sky, and told Joe to look up. When Joe did, Oliver threw the brick onto his foot. Joe started hopping around, accidentally fell against a window, and went right through it.

Oliver went to help and ended up ripping his pants (toward the people who are watching the movie.)

As they left, Joe said, "We have to find an apartment."

"That's right, we have to find an apartment," Stan said.

"Would you stop saying everything over again?" Oliver asked him, annoyed. He shook his head.

The boys found an apartment on the third floor. Oliver and Stan started telling Joe a couple of things about slapstick. A little bit later as Joe was looking out a window, Stan got a chair and went over by him and knocked him out the window. Stan started crying as he saw Joe hanging from a flagpole.

Oliver looked out the window at Joe and told Stan to go get a car while he got a ladder. Stan drove up, and Oliver put the ladder on top of the car. Something happened, and Stan drove away, leaving Joe and Oliver (who had gone up to get Joe) stuck on the ladder. Stan drove up onto the sidewalk, and people were jumping everywhere, even through windows. One man even jumped right into a cake that was in a bakery!

Meanwhile, Stan was crying all over the place, and they knocked a cop right on his can. Finally, the car hit the side of a building, sending Joe flying into a pet store and Oliver into a puddle of mud. Oliver lay there and played with his fingers while Joe landed head-first in a big bowl of dog food. Stan came over, and Oliver and Joe just looked at him.

"Another fine mess you've gotten me into!" Oliver said to him.

Stan began crying again. Suddenly the car started by itself. "Don't say anything, just help us!" Joe said. Stan went over to help Oliver out of the mud but only ended up knocking him right back into the mud.

When they got back to the apartment, Joe said, "This is really good, guys. This is the slapstick I have been writing!"

"Don't worry, Joe. You'll get there," Stan said to him.

"That is a very smart thing to say," Oliver said to Stan, who nodded. "hey, I know some firemen. Let's go find them."

On the way, Joe saw a quarter, and when he went to pick it up, he got all wet from the water cleaning the streets.

"It feels good to see somebody else get it one in a while!" Oliver said to him. Meanwhile Stan smiled broadly.

"You guys are friends like I've never seen. God bless you, Oliver and Stan. I just don't know what to say." Joe said as he turned to them.

Then Oliver said, "On with the slapstick!"

They reached the firehouse, and the alarm went off. Joe started driving the fire truck to the fire. As Stan saw exactly where the fire was, the boys pulled up there.

Oliver went for the hose, but it wasn't long enough. So Stan started getting pails of water to put the fire out. Joe got the ladder and put it against the house. As Oliver was trying to fix the hose, the fire burned his butt.

Stan was fooling around near the ladder that Joe was on, and accidentally knocked the ladder the other way, sending Joe through another window. Stan started to cry and jump all over the place. Oliver had to stick his butt into a barrel of water to cool it down.

When they got back to the apartment, Oliver said, "You guys can't do anything right! This is another fine mess you've gotten me into!"

Stan kept crying. "It was not my fault!"

The boys decided to get some rest before planning their next slapstick adventure.

"I have a friend who needs a piano delivered," Oliver told them. So they went to the store to get the piano. When they got to the stairs, they noticed that the place they had to take it to was way up there. Halfway up Stan had to tie his shoe. As he stood up, he hit Joe with his head, and Joe lost his balance and tripped, and the piano started on its way down the stairs, rolling over Oliver's foot. It kept going until it was out the door and in the street. Stan and Joe took the piano back to the top of the stairs, as Oliver was coming up. A bee began to buzz around them, and Joe tried to slap at it, but he missed the bee and slapped Stan instead, and the piano rolled back down the stairs and over Oliver. Again Stan began to cry, and Oliver played with his fingers.

Joe told Laurel and Hardy that in his time, he used to make pizza when he was young. So they went to a pizza parlor. Joe was showing Oliver how to make pizza, and Stan was in the back, getting ready to mix the pizza dough. Joe told Stan to make sure that the machine was set on number one, not number two.

In front Oliver was getting ready to put a pizza in the oven. As he heard an unfamiliar sound, he turned around and accidentally threw the pizza right out of his hands. It landed on Joe's head, and the sauce and cheese dripped all over him. "Here's a fine mess you've gotten all over me!" Joe said.

Joe went into the back and asked Stan, "Are you ready?" Stan was turning the wheel on the mixer. He hit number two, so when Joe turned it on, flour went all over the place. Stan stood there crying and saying that it was an accident.

Oliver came into the back and said, "Look at this place. Just look at the mess you made!"

Stan was still crying and scratching his head. "You can't do anything right," Oliver and Joe both said.

They went back to the apartment and Joe said, "This has been great, guys! I learned a lot in the slapstick world."

The boys were really happy. "It's time to take you back, Joe," they told him.

"I am going to miss you guys," Joe said as he gave them a big hug. Stan was really crying now. Then Joe asked, "Will I ever see you guys again?"

"You never know," Oliver told him. "Just keep dreaming."

When Joe got back, he heard his mother knocking at the door. "Joe, there are two men here to see you," she said.

Joe went downstairs, and the two men asked if he was Joe Marsh. "That's me," he told them. They said they were from Hollywood and they wanted to talk to him about his stories.

Joe and his mother left for Hollywood immediately. Joe's mother was so happy her son's hard work might finally pay off.

All of a sudden Laurel and Hardy popped their heads through the floor. "We can be proud of Joe. He's going to do fine," Oliver said to Stan.

"Yes, he's going to do fine," Stan replied.

"Won't you shut up. I just said that!"

This story is dedicated to Laurel and Hardy.

The Hunter of Hunters: the Adventures of Lou and Greta

Lou and Greta were driving down the road through a forest. The weather was rainy, and there was a slight mist in the air, but they didn't mind. Greta had her Juicy Fruits, and Lou had his Cracker Jacks. Lou said to Greta, "Look, I got a good prize this time!"

"What is it, Lou?" Greta asked him.

"It's a clown," Lou told her. "the kind with the balls in its eyes and mouth."

Greta looked at Lou and thought, *What a man my Lou is!* All of a sudden they heard a loud *boom*! "Lou, I think we got a flat!" Greta said to him. Lou stopped the car, got out, and then gave the car a good kick (which didn't do much for his foot). Lou hopped all over the place saying "nuts!"

Greta got out of the car. "Easy, Lou," she said to him. "I like your feet the way that they are!"

Lou just looked at her and said, "yeah, right."

So Greta sat down next to a tree. After a minute she started to hear a noise coming from the woods. "Lou, I hear something!" She cried, causing him to drop the car jack on his foot. As he began to hop around on one foot again, three squirrels appeared. There was a father squirrel accompanied by two daughter squirrels. Greta turned to Lou, and said, "They're cartoons, and we can see them–just like your grandmother could!"

"I guess it runs in the family!" he told her.

Then the father squirrel said, "Yes, we know your grandmother. My name is Walnut, and my girls are Strawberry and Morning Glory."

"Oh, Lou! they're so cute, and their caps and sweatshirts are such a pretty shade of red!" Greta said. Then Walnut told Lou that they needed their help.

"You need our help for what?" Lou asked the squirrel, "to scare hunters out of the forest? You want us to kill them?" Lou asked.

"No," said Walnut. "We just want to scare them out of the forest."

"We have to help them, Lou," Greta said.

"Okay," said Lou, looking like a real tough guy. "Sure, we can do that."

"What a man!" Greta said about Lou, who only looked at and shook his head.

Strawberry pulled on Lou's pant leg and asked him if she and her sister could have some Cracker Jacks. "Sure you can," Lou told her, "and look, you can have this prize!"

"Look, Morning Glory, a clown!" Strawberry said to her sister.

Then Lou said to Walnut, "Well, what's the plan?"

"Well," Walnut said, "Greta and my girls will go looking for the hunters while we get all of my raccoon friends to help."

About a half an hour passed, and they met back at the same place. Greta told them that there were about five hunters making camp not too far from where they were. Meanwhile, the raccoons were pulling on Lou's pants, asking for Cracker Jacks. Lou turned to Greta and said, "Can you get some more Cracker Jacks out of the car?"

"Anything for my man!" Greta said as she turned to Lou.

"She must love you a lot," Walnut told Lou, who only replied, "Yeah, yeah, yeah."

That night as the hunters went to sleep, the army of raccoons was hiding around them. Lou told the animals that he had a whistle and asked them to wait until he blew it before they attacked. Lou turned to Walnut and asked him, "Will they see you as you are–-cartoons?"

"Just until we scare them out of the woods," the squirrel told him.

When you blew the whistle, the raccoons scampered across everything, leaving little footprints. The hunters woke up and started running all over the camp, tripping over everything. One of the hunters yelled out, "It's an army of cartoon raccoons!" as he was running in his shorts. Two of the other hunters ran into each other and knocked themselves out. Greta and Lou just laughed as Strawberry and Morning Glory pulled on Lou's pants again for more Cracker Jacks. In the meantime, the raccoons had eaten all of the hunters' food and said goodbye as they disappeared into the mist.

"Come with me," Walnut said to Lou. "I have a lot of turkey friends, and Greta and my two girls can look for more hunters!"

"Lou," the girls said, "do you have any more Cracker Jacks?"

"sorry, girls. You ate them all," Lou told them.

"Come with me girls, I have some Juicy Fruits," Greta said to the girls.

That night Lou and Walnut returned with lots of turkeys. They looked over at Greta and the two girls, who were sitting under a tree eating Juicy Fruits.

"Did you find hunters?" Lou asked them.

"Oh, yes! there are about eight of them pitching camp about a half a mile from here," Greta replied.

Everybody made their way to the camp and watched while the hunters ate dinner, waiting for them to go to sleep.

The two girls were lying on top of Greta, and Walnut said to Lou, "They like her a lot.

Lou nodded. He looked at the turkeys and decided it was time for them to start their plan. He blew his whistle, and the turkeys began walking all over the camp and relieving themselves all over everything. Greta and the girls were laughing really hard in between the Juicy Fruits, and Walnut and Lou were laughing too as Lou held Walnut in his arms.

After a little while the noise that the turkeys were making began to awaken the hunters. It was like garage heaven! Everything smelled awful. The hunters couldn't stand the odor. They ran through the forest with flies swarming all over them. The left their tents, clothing, and gear. The only things they took were their guns as they ran to their cars.

"What next?" Lou asked, turning to Walnut.

"Porcupines!" Walnut replied.

"Did you hear that?" Lou asked Greta.

"Yes," she told him as Strawberry and Morning Glory were pulling on her pants, asking for more Juicy Fruits.

Greta and the two squirrel girls left to find more hunters while Lou and Walnut went to find the porcupines. About twenty minutes later Greta and the girls were back waiting for them. All of a sudden lots of porcupines start coming, followed closely by Lou and Walnut. Lou and Greta went into the hunters' camp and hid their guns. Then Lou went to Walnut and asked if they were ready. Walnut said, "Yes," and Lou blew his whistle. Suddenly the porcupines charged the camp! The hunters were covered with needles!

"I've never seen anything like this," Greta said to Lou. "The hunters are pulling pins out of each others' butts! Some of them are even climbing trees!"

As the hunters were running to their cars, they could hear them shouting in pain. The girls were giggling and pulling on Greta's pants again, asking for more Juicy Fruits.

As the porcupines were leaving, Walnut said, "Look, they left food here!"

"You boys go relax, and me and the girls will fix some food to eat," Greta told them.

"If you find any Cracker Jacks," Lou said to Greta, "let me know."

Greta looked at the girls and said, "That's my man!" The girls started giggling again.

Lou began making a campfire. "So you know my grandmother," he said to Walnut.

"Yes," Walnut replied. "All cartoons know her. She is an angel. She is good. She has three cartoons living with her—haunted cartoons, that is. They fit the house perfect!"

"I've got to go see her." Lou said.

As they finished eating, Lou said, "It will be light in about four hours, so let's get some sleep."

Lou went over to lie down next to Greta, but the girls were already there. So he just smiled at her and gave her a kiss. The giggles started all over again. Lou looked at the girls and said, "What next?"

"Well, I have a lot of friends who are skunks . . . ." Walnut replied.

Lou said, "This is going to be really smelly for the hunters!"

Greta and the girls set out to look for more hunters. Before they left, Lou pulled a hairpin from Greta's hair.

Greta and the girls found about nine hunters camping near a river. Greta turned to the girls and said, "You go get them, and I'll wait here for you."

So Strawberry and Morning Glory started to go get the others, but then they saw Lou coming, and they laughed hysterically because he had a hairpin on his noise.

When they got to where Greta was, she began to laugh at Lou also, but then she sniffed the air and pulled a hairpin from her hair to clip it over her nose too.

Lou looked at Walnut and then blew his whistle. The skunks attacked. The hunters did not believe it. They took off their shirts and waved them around in the air with one hand while the other hand held their noses. Three of them jumped into the river and started swimming across it while the others ran through the woods with the skunks right behind them.

Lou, Greta, Walnut, and the girls watched as the skunks lost themselves in the woods. "Well, we gotta go, but me and Greta will come back," said Lou, "and when we do, we'll bring you some Cracker Jacks and Juicy Fruits."

They walked them to their car and waved good-bye. As they drove away, Lou asked Greta, "Could we check the glove compartment?" Greta opened it. "Look! a box of Cracker Jacks!" she said.

"I knew I had one more box!" he said.

As he began to eat, Greta looked at Lou and said, "What a man my Lou is!"

Indefinite Bus

Joe was getting ready to go to work at the bus transportation headquarters of New York City. As he left, he looked at his history books before taking one more drink from his coffee cup. *Boy I make good coffee.*

He arrived at the bus depot, checked in, and started on his normal route. Most of the people who got on the bus had known Joe for years. At one stop two ladies got on. They were about sixty years old and had know Joe for forty years.

"Hi, Joe," said Sarah.

Joe said, "Hello, ladies."

Sarah said, "Are we going to have a good drive today, Joe?"

"Sure we will," Joe replied. "I will give you a ride like you never felt before! An hour later there were about thirty people in the bus. Joe picked up his microphone, so that the people know where they are and where he is. Joe made his normal right turn, and all of a sudden lightning started flashing in all shades and colors.

In a matter of seconds Joe and the people looked around in shock. For some reason the bus was sitting in the jungle. Joe turned back to the people, "Okay, folks, I don't know what has happened here, but let's try to think on this."

All of a sudden a brontosaurus came walking through the bus like a ghost, and two baby brontosauruses come walking through too, with their heads sticking up through the bus floor.

Joe picked up his microphone and said, "All right, did everybody see that?"

One kid yelled out, "This is better than being at an amusement park!"

Joe started telling the people to be calm. He opened the bus door and tried to step out, but there was nothing there. A man behind him, Bill, grabbed ahold of Joe before he fell into nowhere. Joe looks at Bill. "We must be going through some kind of time barrier or dimension."

Joe looked straight ahead as a giant pteranodon flew toward them. All the passengers huddled behind Joe and Bill and watched as the pteranodon soared right through them.

"Wow!" said one kid. One lady was getting pretty shaken up, so Joe decided to keep driving, and they were amazed at the kinds of prehistoric animals outside the bus. On one side of the bus was a pentaceratops, and then they saw a herd of phenacodus drinking water from a lake. Joe started driving the bus through the trees and dinosaurs and made a right-hand turn, and the colored lightning started all over again.

It is now 68 A.D., and they are watching Nero honor his army in Rome. Sarah turned to Joe. "Is that Nero?" she asked.

Joe said, "I don't know. I was born in Brooklyn, New York."

Joe continued driving through everything. As they drive through Nero, Nero's body passed right through Sarah, and Joe joked, "Sarah, at your age!" Joe said to himself, *It seems a joke here and there could help the stress,* so he parked the bus for a while and started talking to the people. "I guess time is playing some kind of game with us, but we are going to get out of this some way." As they looked out the window, they saw the burning city of Rome.

"This is unbelievable!" Bill exclaimed. Roman people were running right through the bus and the people on the bus. Joe started driving again and makes a right turn, and the colored lighting started again.

This time they found themselves in an ocean between two vessels. One kid said that one of the ships was a pirate ship because of the three skulls on a black flag and that the other was British.

Bill said, "We must be in the Jamaican waters."

"And it must be around 1670," Joe added. As the two vessels got within cannon range, the cannons fired from both sides, and the cannonballs shot through the bus and people. One kid yelled,"Wow! I just got a cannon ball right through me."

As the passengers watched in fascination, pirates came swinging through the bus to get on the British ship. They heard the dirty talk of the pirates.

Sarah said, "they are not gentleman at all!" Everybody started laughing.

The pirates cut the British sailors to pieces. As the pirates took over the ship, the people watched helplessly as they threw the British in the ocean. They heard one pirate say, Captain Mogan, what shall we do with the captain?"

Mogan yelled, "Throw him over."

Joe picked up his microphone. "Okay, people, is this better than going to the movies or what?"

"One kid said, "Let's go!" Joe makes another right-hand turn, but nothing happened, so he decided to turn left. *Now,* Joe said to himself, *even on water I can drive.* He makes a left-hand turn, and nothing happens. Joe turned around and said, "Maybe we should just keep going right. We've only got 300 more years to go. I mean, *I think,* we are getting near to our time." Joe made a right turn. The colored lightning started again, but it was dark outside.

Bill said, "Look there are mountains out there."

Joe said, "It must be nighttime wherever we are now."

There were about eight kids on the bus, and they all had their lunches with them. They decided to eat and then try to sleep for a few hours.

Joe started talking to some woman and told her, "I never seen you on the bus before. What is your name?"

"Cindy," she replied, "And yours is Joe." Cindy told Joe, " I love this. This is great!"

Joe said, "Yeah, me too, but I don't want the people to know that."

As the sun began to rise, most of the people got up to stretch their muscles. Bill said, "Look it is the Wild West."

Joe said, "Yeah, you are right."

Bill said, "I grew up out here."

Joe said, "I think we got a dust storm coming from the other way."

One boy called out, "It is Indians!" as the people watch thousands of them are coming in their direction.

Sam said to Joe, "I think this is Little Big Horn Canyon."

Joe said, "General Custer and the Seventh Cavalry were killed here."

As the Indians raced nearer, Sam said, "Look! That is Crazy Horse."

As all the Indians started through the bus, Joe said, I wish they could see us. I could tell them that we are all Americans." Then Joe said, "Well, we can make a right turn now or follow the. What do you think?" Even the older people and Sarah wanted to follow them, so Joe asked why. Sarah said that her grandfather was in the Seventh Cavalry.

"Okay," Joe said. "Let's go after them." Joe parked atop a hill and saw the Seventh Cavalry led by a man with long blonde hair.

One kid said, "That is Custer!" As the Indians attacked, they watched the Seventh Cavalry fall all over everywhere. This continued for an hour. As the Indians prepared to overrun them, Joe said, "There must be seventy soldiers left." The people were astonished to witness something that had happened in their own country. As they were overrun, the Indians just kept on going as the people from the bus watched in shock. All they saw standing was the Seventh Cavalry flag.

Joe started the bus and drove away. Everybody was real silent. Joe made a right turn. The colored lightning started and they were back in New York City. Joe looked at his watch and realized it was the same time as when they had left. He turned around to the passengers and said, "There is no way I am going to tell anybody about this. They will think we are nuts!"

Everybody agrees not to say anything. Joe dropped off everyone except Cindy. Joe asked, "Where can I drop you off?"

Cindy said, "I can tell you are going back, Joe, and I want to come."

Joe asked her if she was sure. Cindy said, "I am sure.

They picked up food and drinks and sleeping bags. Joe started driving down the street, and it happened for both of them. The colored lightning started, and Joe and Cindy began living their dream.

Leo the Lion: Superhero

In 1825 John Seal stood on a hill, drawing maps of the stars. He was always amazed at the sight of them. He was a young man. As he was laying out his map, two flashes of light from the constellation Leo hit his eyes. He fell backwards, looked up, and two more lights hit him as he got to his knees. The last two lights sent him onto his stomach. He turned his head, and a flash of pure yellow light hit his head. He looked up at the sky and screamed as Leo the Lion came out of him. John looked at the lion and wondered what was happening to him.

"Relax," said Leo. "I have been watching you draw your stars, and I like what I see." then he told John he was going to take him into the stars and teach him and give him honor.

"Walk into me," Leo told John. As he did, Leo left like a shooting star to the heavens. Once they were there, Leo began to teach John about his destiny. He told him that he would live forever and that his destiny was to help people in harm's way.

"Your power is in this ring," Leo told him. "When you start to run, rub this ring and say my name, and I will come out of you."

John was amazed. He was also amazed by the way the other stars communicated with each other. John turned to Leo. "How will I live? You need money to live in my world."

"That's been handled. I will drop you back onto Earth when the California gold rush is just about to begin. You will have what you need to on forever," Leo explained to him. Then he added, "Remember, rub the ring and say my name."

Leo returned John to earth five days before the first man struck gold and showed him where his share would be. Two months went by, and John had everything he needed. One day he heard noises coming from another camp. He was horrified to see his neighbor being beat up by four men. John started running and rubbed his ring, which could never be removed now, and called out, "Leo." He then turned into Leo and started beating the four men up but did not kill them. As Leo looked into the man's eyes, the man saw the brightest yellow he had ever seen. Leo took off, and the man just looked down and shook his head, thinking to himself that he couldn't believe what he had just see.

The years passed by, and it was 1901. John had a nice pad in New York, overlooking Central Park. His supernatural power had become even greater. He could now hear things at great distances and could leap to great heights. He stood by his window, looking out, when all of a sudden, he heard the sound of a woman screaming. He moved all the way back against the wall. Then as he started to run, he rubbed his ring and said, "Leo." As he turned into Leo, he leapt right out the window, which was at least a six-story drop. He landed on his paws and started tracking the screams. They were coming from Central Park.

There he saw two men trying to rape a woman. When they saw Leo, one of them started to run, and the other started to climb a tree. Leo caught the one who was running away and sent him flying into a tunnel wall. Leo went over to the man who was in the tree, and using his super strength, he pulled the tree backwards and let it go just like a slingshot, sending the man flying into a pond headfirst.

The woman was in shock, not so much because of the attack but because of what she had just witnessed. Leo looked at the woman with his bright yellow eyes and then took off running through the park. When the police got there, the woman started telling Sergeant Hayward what she had seen. Sergeant Hayward thought to himself that it was not the first time that someone had reported an incredible rescue by a lion.

As Leo changed back into John, he heard fire alarms going off. As he got to the fire, he saw two children on top of a building, with a lot of panicking people standing around. They were too high for the ladders to reach! Just as John turned into Leo, the children fell off the building as they were trying to edge away from the flames. Leo caught them just in time. He set them down gently and disappeared just as quickly as he had come. Nobody said a single word, but they all looked at each other in disbelief.

When John got back home, he just lay on his bed and closed his eyes.

In 1985 John was still living next to Central Park. One day he was looking through his mail when he realized that he was very lonely. He was human and had human emotions. He then thought that he didn't want to start something that he couldn't finish, so he tried to ignore the feelings and went back to reading his mail. As he opened one envelope, he found an invitation to a formal party that was being thrown the next night.

The following night as John arrived at the party, he saw many important people there. John was standing over by the punch bowl when a woman named Kim came over to him and said, "Hi."

"Oh, hello," said John. "Are you enjoying yourself?"

"A little," Kim answered. "there are a lot of people here with their noses in the air though."

"Well, those are the kind of people that gather at a party like this," John told her. Then he asked, "Where do you work?"

"Oh, I work for a lawyer. And you?"

"I like to write stories."

"Oh, how nice!" said Kim.

Suddenly John touched his ear. He turned to Kim and said, "Listen, I have to do something. Can you wait here for me?"

"Sure," she said. "I'll be here."

A bank just down the block was being robbed. So John began to run. As he ran he touched his ring and said, "Leo," transforming into the lion once again.

Leo went right through the doors into the bank. The three bank robbers couldn't believe what they were seeing. Leo wasted no time. He got ahold of the three men, tied them up, and hung them by their feet. As he left the bank he realized many people had seen him.

When the police got there, they couldn't understand how the bank robbers had gotten up there. "The people are saying it was a lion," said one officer to another.

Captain Bock knew it was not the first time there had been a sighting of a lion. He had read reports about a mysterious lion from many many years ago.

Word soon reached the party about what had happened at the bank with the lion. Kim asked John, "Did you finish what you had to do?"

"Yeah, it's all finished."

Kim looked at John and began to wonder if he knew more than he had said.

John interrupted her thoughts. "Listen," he said, "would you like to have dinner tomorrow?"

"Yes, I would," she told him and gave him her address and phone number.

"I will see you tomorrow night," she said as she turned to leave.

At work Kim started using her computer to find out more about John Seal. She punched up something that she could hardly believe. John Seal had disappeared in 1825! She sat back in her chair with her hand over her mouth.

That night at dinner they ordered a bottle of fine wine. Kim asked John where he was from.

"Washington state," John told her.

"So do your parents still live there?" Kim asked.

"Oh, no. They died when I was young."

"When were you young, John?" she asked.

"Say that again?" John asked, looking kind of baffled.

"Oh, never mind. The medication I'm on makes me act kind of stupid." John looked deep into her eyes. Then she asked him if he had ever been married.

"No, have you?" John replied.

"No, I've never been married either," she told him.

So they finished up dinner, and John took Kim home. She gave him a goodnight kiss and asked him to call her the next day. "You bet," John said, and went home.

Later, at home Leo appeared to John. "I know about your problem. There is one way that she can live forever with you without the powers you have, but for it to work, you have to make sure that she loves you," Leo explained to John.

The next day John went to Kim's house again. Kim opened the door. "We have to talk," he told her. "I know you think that I'm more than I appear to be, so I want you to sit down and watch."

Then he moved back and began to run. He rubbed his ring and said the word "Leo," and turned into the lion. Kim couldn't believe it! She walked up to Leo and said, "John, what happened? I knew there was something, but this!"

Leo turned back into John. "You're the only one that knows about this," he told her. Then he told her how it all started.

Weeks passed by, and one day John and Kim were out doing all kinds of things together. As they walked down Forty-second Street, they saw a man holding a gun to a police officer's head. John turned to Kim and said, "Go home, and I'll see you there."

Kim watched John change into Leo and then went home. Leo got behind the man with the gun and knocked him out with a swat of his paw. Then he handed the man over to the officer and ran down Forty-second Street. His paws were so powerful that people could hear the sound they made against the ground.

Before John got to Kim's house, he picked up a bouquet of flowers. Kim came to the door wearing something so sexy that John dropped the flowers and just stood there looking like a little boy. Kim took John's hand and led him into the bedroom. John knew then that she loved him and that he loved her.

After they finished their love making, John turned to Kim and said, "You will live forever like me, but if you lose your love for me, then you will grow old."

"I will never lose my love for you, John."

"That's good," said John. "That's real good."

The next day it was all over the papers. Everyone was calling him a superhero.

The next day John and Kim went to city hall to get married. Kim was so happy, and John—well, that spoke for itself. Later on at home they watched a special report on the television. Three men were holding forty people hostage on an airplane. "I've got to go!" John said, turning to Kim. She gave him a big kiss and then kissed his ring. John's eyes glowed with pure yellow light.

At the airport the men were demanding five million dollars, or else they would begin killing the hostages. As John turned into Leo, the police saw him coming, and so did the extortionists. Leo stopped in front of the police. He knew that he could not go through the front way.

The police were looking at Leo, and Captain Bock tried talking to him. "If you understand me, shake your head," the Captain said. Leo shook his head. The Captain looked at one of his officers and said, "I guess he understands!" Then he turned to Leo and asked, "What can we do?"

Leo got beneath the airplane and broke through the plane floor and pulled some of the men out. Then he went into the plane through the hole, got another one of the men, and put him through the window. The last man shot at Leo and hit him, but the wound healed instantly. Leo went over and got the man and dragged him down the airplane stairs feet first. All the people were cheering him as he ran away.

"I wonder who he is," said one officer to Captain Bock.

"It's better that we don't know," the Captain said. "But I do know one thing—he's on our side."

When John got home, Kim threw her arms around him and gave him a big hug. John looked down at Kim and asked, "How about a vacation?"

"I've already packed," she told him.

As John closed his door, he looked up, and his eyes turned pure yellow. Dedicated to all Leos around the world.

Truck Stop

In the year 1939 Joe and Nancy Cobb opened a restaurant and gas station four miles from Bakersfield, California. Over the years, they became known to truck drivers as "Ma" and "Pa."

They heard all the outrageous stories the truck drivers drummed up—fights, women problems, strange things in the sky, and strange things on the roads.

In 1949 Ma and Pa were cooking, getting ready for business. "Would you like some pancakes before we open, Pa?"

"Okay," said Pa, "and some toast."

As they finished up breakfast, the truck drivers started rolling in. Ma went over to the juke box and put on a Perry Como song. Pa yelled for her to put on a Doris Day next as the first truck driver entered.

"Hi, Ma. Hi, Pa," the trucker said to them.

"Hello, Joe," Ma said. "How is everything?"

"You know, Ma, the same old stuff. Except that I have to take my dog to the vet," he told her.

"What's the problem, Joe?" Ma asked.

"Well," Joe said, "he was acting strange. He was trying to bite things that weren't even there.

"Is that right?" said Pa. "Maybe there was a full moon."

Ma turned to Joe. "What will it be?"

"Oh, throw on a couple of eggs and bacon and coffee," Joe told her.

Ma turned to Pa and said, "It's going to be a long day." All of a sudden they heard a noise coming from outside. There, a truck driver was pulling his girlfriend out of his truck. They heard him say: "You better go to a doctor! I'm tired of you telling me you see things that aren't there!"

Ma turned to Pa. "It's Frank and Lois!" she said.

"I guess Lois is seeing things again," Pa said.

Frank and Lois came into the restaurant. "Hi, everybody," said Frank.

"Problems, Frank?" Ma asked him.

"Yeah," he told her. "Lois saw something that is the pits."

"What's that?" Pa asked.

"Well, as we were driving, I was taking a nap. Lois tells me that she saw a man running in his shorts, and three women were chasing him with whips," Frank told them.

"Can you beat that!" Ma said. "Well maybe she did. These days anything can happen!"

Joe smiled. Then he said, "One more cup of coffee, Ma, and I gotta hit the road. I got to get to L.A. with this shipment I'm hauling."

So Ma turned to Lois. "Was the man good-looking?" she asked.

"I couldn't see his face, just his back," Lois answered.

"What were the women wearing?"

"That was the strange thing," Lois told her. "Two of them were wearing cowboy clothing, but the third one was completely naked except for an army helmet."

Frank looked at Pa and shook his head. Then he walked over to the juke box and put on Nat King Cole's "Unforgettable."

Within an hour truckers had filled the little restaurant. Ma and Pa's son, Hank, came into work. "Any good stories today, Pa?" he asked him.

"Yeah," he told him. "Lois over there has a real pit of a story."

Just then, Max, a guy with incredibly unbelievable stories walked in. "Hi!" Ma said to Max.

"Hello, Pa. Hi, Ma," he said to them.

"Well, what will you have?" asked Ma.

"Oh, give me a grilled cheese and fries," Max answered.

"So," Pa said, "what's new, Max?"

"Well, two nights ago," Max began, "as I was driving, I saw a spaceship at the side of the road, and there were two aliens boxing!"

"Boxing!" said Hank. "That must've been a good fight!"

"Did you see who won?" Pa asked.

"No," Max said. "I wanted to stop, but I knew that I might scare them away, and I didn't want to ruin the fight."

Here's your grilled cheese, Max." Ma said. She looked at Pa and rolled her eyes.

Another truck driver named John walked in. "Hi, John. How are you?" Ma asked him.

"Not so good," he answered.

"What's wrong?" Pa asked.

"My girlfriend ran off with another truck driver."

"There are more out there," Pa said.

Ma turned to Pa and said, "There you are, a 'Dear John' letter."

"A couple of police officers stopped by to get some coffee. As they walked in, they saw John and sat down next to him.

"I wonder what's wrong with him," said one cop to the other.

"Who knows when it comes to truck drivers!" said the second officer.

It was getting late in the afternoon, so Ma, Pa, and Hank began preparing for the dinner rush. They had a meatloaf special that night. After a little while Ma heard Pa, who was out back smoking his pipe, call her. She went out and Pa said, "Look at that! There's that man running in his shorts with three women chasing after him!"

"Well, I guess she really saw it!" Ma said.

Pa kind of laughed. Then he said, "The one without any clothes on isn't bad!"

"come on, let's go get ready for the rush."

During dinner a lady truck driver named Ann came in. She was always smoking a cigar and had tattoos covering her arms. She greeted them as she walked in.

"Hi, Ann. Get any lately?" Ma said.

"Oh, yes," Ann said. "I was in L.A., hanging out in a bar, and this man kept looking at me. So I got up and grabbed him and took him in the back of my truck. He was all right, but I've had better."

Pa looked at Ma and said, "Poor man!"

"Now, now," said Ma. "It's not your business to judge!"

As more people started coming in, Hank started talking to a girl sitting next to Max. The girl was telling Max that she loved hanging out where truckers were.

"Why is that?" Max asked her.

"Well," said the girl, "I like that macho thing."

"Oh, really," Hank said to her, as a truck driver put a Bing Crosby song on the juke box and started talking to Ma.

"How are you, Ma?" he asked.

"Fine," she answered him. "And you?"

"Oh, not too bad."

"How's life on the road?"

"Strange," said the truck driver, whose name was Sam. He was one of only a few truck drivers who didn't have crazy stories to tell. This day, however, he said to Ma, "You're not going to believe this, but today I saw a man running in his shorts with three women running after him with whips. One of them was totally naked with an army helmet on!"

"Me and Pa saw the same thing about an hour ago," Ma told him.

Sam just shook his head and said, "Strange."

"So, what'll it be, Sam?" Ma asked him.

"Steak, potatoes, and a beer."

"Okay, Sam," she said as she went to get his order.

Meanwhile, the girl Hank was talking to was telling him how she liked her men to dress.

"How is it that you like them to dress?" he asked.

"With nothing on!" she said.

"Well, I don't think a man would want to walk around with no clothes on!"

Just while we're at home. I like to watch." she told him.

"Okay," Hank said, "but I have to get back to work now."

Pa had overheard the conversation and whispered to Hank, "go for it!"

"Pa, I don't think I want to walk around the house naked!" Hank said.

"Why not?" Pa asked.

"As long as nobody else sees you!" Hank said as the girl looked him up and down.

Pa started talking to another truck driver, who began telling him about something that he had seen on the road. "Well, there was a man and a woman. The woman was on the man's back, and she was slapping him on the butt saying, 'come on, boy, come on! Only three more miles, and we'll be there!'" Then the truck driver, whose name was Mike, told them, "then I drove three more miles after I had passed them, and there was nothing out there but desert!"

"Now that's very strange," said Pa, and the truck driver agreed with him.

Meanwhile, Ma was talking to a different trucker, who was telling her a really strange story. He said that as he was driving, he saw three people on the road fighting with each other. "I pulled over," he said, "and asked if everything was okay. The three people turned to me and said, 'Get the hell out of here!' Just then two cars pulled up, and eight men got out wearing all-white clothing and black hats that were at least four feet high! Well," he went on, "they got the people and put them in the cars and took off."

"Well, what did you think of it?" Ma asked him.

"You see, that was the funny thing. As I was driving away, I looked through my mirror, and the two cars just disappeared!"

"Is that right?" Ma asked in disbelief.

"That's right!" the truck driver told her. Meanwhile, the girl, Debbie, was still giving Hank the eye. It was getting late, and Ma and Pa started cleaning up. Hank went over to Debbie and asked her if she would like to go out.

"Oh, yes," she said. "You can come over to my house and walk around naked!"

So Hank and Debbie left and Ma and Pa told them to have fun. As Ma and Pa were closing up, they saw the man running in his shorts, with the three women still chasing him.

Red Hot Devils

In the heavens, Lucifer, one of the Lord's angels, plotted against him. And so the angels of the Lord took Satan to the tunnels of Mars. Over hundreds of years, life developed on Mars and Satan created an army of red hot devils. Satan planned to destroy all life on the planet Mars by sending out his red hot devils.

Their power had no limit. They destroyed life on Mars completely, blowing everything up with their pitchforks.

The explosions blew rocks everywhere. Some of them even blew out of the atmosphere of Mars and floated through space. Some of the rocks found their way to Earth, carrying life forms. Millions of years passed by. Meanwhile, Satan and his red hot devils find their way to Earth and live deep within the earth's core, where they remain and wait. Many, many years pass by.

Now, in the year 1948, in Washington, D.C., Father Williams was working in the garden behind his church. Father Williams was a very good man. As well as his work in the church, Father Williams helped people in need whenever he can. Children loved him, and he could often be seen joining in games with young people.

As he dug into the ground to plant a rose bush, he heard somebody call, "Father!"

"Yes, I am here!" he called out. "In the back. In the garden!" He looked around, but didn't see anyone. He began to think he must have imagined it.

Then he heard: "Father Williams, behind you." Slowly he turned around. Amazed, he falls to his knees. Before him, he saw a brightly glowing tree that did not burn. In it he saw the spirit of the Lord.

"Behold, my son," said the voice of the Lord. "Rise, my son, for there is something you must do." The Lord told Father Williams of Lucifer (Satan) and his evil plots to destroy the planet Earth and kill every living creature.

In despair Father Williams asked the Lord, "But how can Satan and his kingdom be stopped, my Lord?"

"Thou shall tell all thy people that every single weapon shall be immersed in the essence of pure garlic, for it is pure and it will cleanse. This is how Satan can be vanquished. Although weapons are evil, it must be done," the Lord explained to him. "Now go, and tell them as I have instructed you."

Slowly, the bright light faded, and the image of the Lord disappeared. Tears fell from the eyes of the good Father.

At the Department of Defense in Washington, D.C., Major Lee called out, "Captain Baker, sir, the radar is picking something up. I don't know what it is."

Captain Baker came over to look at the screen with the major. "What is it, Major Lee?" the captain asked.

"Captain, sir, it appears to be about six hundred objects flying out of Mount Helen, Sir," said the major.

"What kind of objects, major?'

Bringing the computer image closer, so they could see more clearly, Major Lee said, "I don't believe it, sir, but they appear to be about four feet long and carrying sharp objects!"

Captain Baker watched the screen, amazed. He went into his office, trying to understand what it could be when one of his privates entered.

"Sir," said the private, "we have just received word that a British warship was destroyed by some sort of laser beam. We are analyzing right now."

"Get Captain Block on the phone!" the captain ordered.

Meanwhile reports of strange sightings of little red devils carrying pitchforks were coming in from everywhere. Major Lee showed these to Captain Baker.

"Is this a joke?!" the captain asked.

"No joke, sir. These reports are coming in world wide. Whatever we are dealing with here, sir, is unlike anything we've ever known before," the major told him. "Also, sir, there is someone here to see you. It's a priest. He says it is very important."

"A priest? Well, why not. Show him in, Major."

A few minutes later Major Lee entered Captain Baker's office with Father Williams. "Well, what can I do for you, Father?" the captain asked.

The father began to tell the captain everything, and Captain Baker could see that Father Williams was sincere. The captain leaned back in his chair and lit a cigar. "Father, what you're telling me, it's unbelievable, yet that's exactly what seems to be happening, isn't it? So what can we do? Bring out our troops? Concentrate our forces?"

"None of that will destroy our enemy," the father told him. "there is only one thing that will work. Every weapon must be dipped in pure garlic. I know you are a man of science, but we are not fighting anything scientific. We are fighting Satan, Captain."

"Well, then," said Captain Baker, "let's do it." He turned to the major and said, "Get me the president on the phone. Now! Let's get things started."

Meanwhile, the red hot devils brought havoc and disaster to China. They destroyed the Great Wall with their pitchforks. People who tried to climb over the Great Wall were melting from the burning rays coming from their pitchforks.

Russia was also taking quite a beating. Nothing was spared! Planes, buildings, and warships were destroyed as the rays from their pitchforks blasted everywhere. The rays were hitting the people as well, causing them to melt.

Father William's advice was spread all over the world as the only chance for victory, and every single country in the world had their men dip every weapon into pure garlic.

In Japan the red devils were coming out of Mount Fuji, causing it to erupt and bringing the ocean to a boil around the coast. The red hot devils were bringing disaster everywhere!

Sailing across the Pacific Ocean, the navy began to fight back using their weapons that had been dipped in pure garlic. As the devils were hitting the sailors with their pitchfork rays, the sailors launched their attack.

The plan was working! The red hot devils began to turn to sand as soon as they were hit!

In New York the red hot devils were running wild, striking people with their pitchforks. The New York Police Department was ready, and they fought back, sending out every single officer with a weapon first prepared in pure garlic. The men were hitting their targets, and the red devils turned to sand and fell from the sky. Captain Baker and Father Williams began boarding a warship. "You know, Father, you don't have to come," said Captain Baker.

"My son," said the father, "I am going."

In the air, war planes were doing very well throughout the world. One red hot devil got a plane over Central Park.

In Paris a plane crashed into the Eiffel Tower. Back in Washington, D. C. The president was on the phone with other world leaders. On the coast of England the red hot devils blew Big Ben to pieces, but the English were retaliating. Red hot devils were falling from the sky everywhere. On the coast of California the military was holding its ground. Three red hot devils flew over the golden Gate Bridge and destroyed it. A soldiers who was a really marksman shot all three, sending them right into the bay. In Africa the tribes were doing a great job with their spears. They lined up and threw them right into the red devils. In New the York bay two hot devils headed for the Statue of Liberty, but the coast guard zoomed right in and stopped them. A mile off the coast of California, the people on the warship that Father Williams was on watched the sky as the red devils fell. Captain Baker turned to the father and asked, "Father, how did you know?"

"I was told of thee," Father Williams replied.

The captain looked at him and smiled. "You did good. There will be a place in mankind for you."

In the heavens the Lord was pleased. He sent three of his best angels to capture Lucifer. They left at the speed of light and went right down to the earth's core. They got Lucifer and took him to Pluto. He went right to its icy center and made this his new kingdom.

Back on Earth all is at peace, so Father Williams goes back home to his garden and plants his rose bush in front of the tree where he had his vision from the Lord.

Myths

Mount Olympus was going through some heavy problems. It seemed Zeus was getting weak. Even with all their wisdom and knowledge Zeus's philosophers could not find the reason. Zeus talked to one of his philosophers, who told him to find out who was causing his loss of power. Pegasus stood by Zeus looking kind of sad, but this was not what was worrying Zeus. He had many of his rival gods, including Cyclops, encased in ice hundreds of years ago. Zeus turned to Pegasus and said, "They could come back to life, and if they did, they would be stronger than ever. I'm also afraid that they would be able to multiply themselves spontaneously."

The year was 1930, and it was a Monday afternoon in the Arctic. An iceberg, at least 300 feet high and 400 feet in width, ripped right in half with Talus's two hands pushing it out. Talus came out and raised his arms to the sky. He was followed by the one-eyed giant Polyphemus. Then out came five Hydras, which were dragons with nine heads. Next came an army of winged creatures, the Harpies. Finally a group of eight with the bodies of lions and the heads and wings of eagles, the gryphons. Zeus turned to Hera and said, "I never dreamed this would happen." Hera told Zeus not to worry. She was sure the philosophers will find the problem and fix it.

Back on earth each Cyclops went his own way. Talus reached the harbor of New York where the military was waiting. Their weapons seemed to have no effect; Talus was too powerful. Talus passed the Statue of Liberty and stopped to look. He walked over to the lady and then turned around and kept walking through the bay. At the Brooklyn Bridge the Coast Guard surrounded him, but they were helpless. A seaman said to his chief officer, "This is unbelievable." A warship got too close to Talus and was smashed by his hand. As he came to the Brooklyn Bridge, he walked right through it, causing cars to tumble into the bay. People on land watched in shock. Talus then climbed onto land and started walking to the United Nations building, stepping on cars and everything else in his path.

The Harpies went through Germany and France. In Paris they swarmed around the towers and the church of Notre Dame, hanging on the statues. Some were down below, chasing the people all around and slapping the backs of their heads. They went into a restaurant and started throwing the people out, before eating their food. Two cops rushed in and were thrown right back through the window by the Harpies. In Germany they surprised everyone. While Hitler was making one of his boring speeches, a Harpie passed in front of him and ripped off his moustache. The Germans began running as the Harpies started slapping them also. Hitler watched wordlessly. Two people sat down to have a glass of wine. The Harpies came, pushed them out of their chairs, and gulped down their wine.

The Hydras didn't waste any time in Japan. With their nine heads, they knocked people down all over the place. The Japanese used everything they could get their hands on to try to stop them. Two men cut off one of the heads and watched in amazement as it instantly grew back. The two men threw down their swords and started running. They were hit with a Hydra's tail, which sent them flying into a building. The Hydras have people wrapped up and hanging around their long necks.

Tribes in Africa tried to protect themselves from the gryphons, fighting with spears and clubs. The women fought alongside the men, but the gryphons were much too powerful. They were able to destroy nearly everything with their beaks. Ten men tried to hold one down, but another gryphon came and killed the men. The people of the tribes started running, chased mercilessly by the gryphons.

In San Francisco there were big problems caused by the one-eyed giant Polyphemus. People watch as Polyphemus started to climb the Golden Gate Bridge. As he climbed to the top, he smashed cars with his club and threw them off the bridge. The army was shooting at him, but didn't do any good at all. It only made him even more mad. While walking through the city, Polyphemus smashed everything in sight with his big club. He smashed a trolley car into pieces. He also picked up cars on the street and threw them at the people.

Back on Mount Olympus Zeus finally had his powers restored thanks to his philosophers. They told Zeus he was betrayed by Andromeda, and he has her encased in a block of ice. Zeus turned to Hera and said he planned to take care of this himself. Hera handed him a red gem. she told him that it would give him the extra power needed to return the Cyclops. Zeus looked at Pegasus and asked if he was ready. Pegasus looked really happy because Zeus was better. He mounted Pegasus and started to descend to Earth.

First Zeus went to Paris. The Harpies saw him coming from the sky. Zeus stretched out his hand and the Harpies disappeared. Next Zeus went to Germany and repeated the situation. Meanwhile Hitler was still standing lock-jawed and alone. In Africa the tribesmen watched with joy as they saw Zeus destroy the gryphons. The Japanese started bowing to Zeus as he demolished the Hydras. They were still bowing after he left. Then in San Francisco the people were shocked when they saw Zeus flying above the Golden Gate Bridge. Polyphemus turned and looked. Then he let out a howling noise as he disappeared.

Finally to New York. Talus was standing next to the United Nations when he looked up and saw Zeus. He tried to hit Zeus with his sword, but he disappeared. The people of New York waved good-bye as Zeus and Pegasus returned home to Mount Olympus.

Zeus and Pegasus arrived home, and all of the gods and goddesses were happy to see them. Zeus went over to a pool of water and saw the planet

Pluto. Frozen there are Talus, Polyphemus, the gryphons, the Harpies, and the Hydras, and Andromeda. Zeus then sat back and sighed, "Finally some peace."

Saint Nick

Six hundred years ago in the Himalayan Mountains, there was a village where a man named Jason lived. One day Jason decided to go on a hike. He especially liked to hike in the wintertime because he loved the fresh clean smell of the winter air and snow. After he had been walking for a while, he came to a snow bank. Suddenly a flash of brilliant colors appeared in the sky above him. Jason heard a loud sound and turned his head. There with a loud crash a man fell into a mound of fallen snow. Jason could hear the man laughing softly and saying, "it's okay, boys."

Curious, Jason walked over to where the man had fallen in the snow. There he saw a man dressed in green clothing with a long beard, as white as the winter snow. Jason was amazed at the sight of a sleigh attached to a team of beautiful reindeer. Standing in front of the man, Jason asked, "are you all right?"

"Yes, yes, my boy," the man replied, brushing snow from his clothing.

"There was nobody around for miles a moment ago," Jason said to him. "And all of a sudden, here you are!"

"Well, my boy, my name is Nick," the man replied. "And you are?"

"Oh, my name is Jason," Jason told him.

"Well, Jason, do you believe that dreams can be real?" Nick asked him.

"Yes, they could happen, I suppose," said Jason.

"Good," said Nick, and he smiled. "But this is not a dream. I come from another dimension."

"Another world?" asked Jason. "That's too hard to believe!"

"No," said Nick. "I'm from this world, just a different dimension. There is something I want to teach you. Will you come with me?"

Jason thought about it for only a moment before he climbed into the beautiful sleigh next to Nick. Turning to Jason, Nick asked, "Ready?"

"I think so," Jason replied.

Then Nick shouted loudly: "Hot cocoa!"

"What? Why did you say 'hot cocoa'?" Jason asked him.

"My reindeer hurry when they hear it. When we're on long trips, they can't wait to get home and have some nice hot cocoa!" Nick explained. Upon hearing the words again, the reindeer went even faster, jerking Jason and Nick along. Faster and faster they raced across the snow, until, just when Jason thought they couldn't possibly go any faster, the first reindeer began to climb high in the sky. Higher and higher it went, pulling up the other reindeer behind it as well.

Jason was scared silly. "Oh my!" he said. "We can't be! We're flying!"

"Don't worry," Nick told him. "Just don't look down!"

Suddenly Nick let out a great big laugh, and Jason couldn't help but laugh too.

Then, just as suddenly, directly in front of them Jason saw a great whirlwind of bright colors swirling beautifully in the sky. "Oh, it's beautiful!" said Jason. Nick just smiled and nodded his head. As they entered the center of the whirlwind, right before Jason's eyes were all kinds of musical instruments—flutes, violins, trumpets, and so many more that he couldn't even count. They were all caught up in the whirlwind and swirling all about.

Where are we going? I've never seen anything like this in my whole life!" Jason shouted.

Nick smiled. "Why, it's magic, my boy!" he said, holding the reins. "Magic, of course!"

Slowly, as they left the whirlwind and the colors began to fade, all the people in this new dimension saw Saint Nick coming, and they hopped into their candy cane sleds to greet him. Nick turned to Jason and said: "Jason, this is how we get everywhere we need to go—in sleds!" As they landed, all of the people gathered around Saint Nick's sled.

"Everybody!" Saint Nick said. "I would like you to meet Jason." There were shouts of hello from everywhere as the people greeted him. Suddenly, like the speed of light, all the reindeer took off again to find some hot cocoa.

"Now it's high time for you to get some rest, and tomorrow I shall tell you why I have brought you here," Saint Nick said to Jason.

"That sounds good," said Jason. "I am very tired."

As Saint Nick took Jason to his room, he agreed. "Yes, you have had quite a day. but that's nothing. Just wait until tomorrow." He smiled and quietly closed the door behind him.

The next morning Jason awoke very early and went for a walk. He couldn't believe his eyes. He was awe struck by all the bright colors and different shapes of the buildings. He walked past a bakery, and in the window he saw all sorts of different-colored cakes and cookies and sweets he had never seen before. He smiled as he noticed the reindeer drinking their hot cocoa. Jason went into the bakery and was walking around looking at all the different things to eat when Saint Nick walked in and said, "Hungry? Have one, anything you like."

Jason picked up a small cake and took a bite. "This is better than anything I've ever had before!" he said.

"I'm glad," said Saint Nick. "Now, it's time for that talk I told you about." He handed Jason a cup of hot cocoa. After they had sat down, Saint Nick asked him, "Do you know the story of Christ?"

"Yes," Jason said. "He was the son of the Lord."

Saint Nick smiled and nodded. "Yes, Jason. That's good. Very good. And in this dimension, we celebrate the 25th of December in honor of the day Christ was born back in your dimension." He went on to say: "I want you to teach them about what you are going to see, but you must not tell them where you've been. They won't believe you at first, so take your time over the years to come. Go walk along our streets and look at everything, for you must remember it well."

Jason left Saint Nick's company to look around on his own. As he walked through the streets, he noticed that they were made of some kind of butter. His feet didn't stick to it, though. It smelled so good! He asked one man, "What is it?"

"Peanut butter," the man said.

He came to another street and noticed that it was called Music Box Street. He looked up the street and saw that there were all kinds of music boxes playing. Jason began to ask questions of anybody that he met. He walked up Jack-in-the-Box Street. On this street he saw all kinds of jack-in-the-boxes, and they were all sounding off, just like the music boxes on the other street were. He couldn't believe his ears.

He went a little farther until he came to a street called "Fruit Place." As he went down this street, he began reaching for some of the fruit that lined the street. There were apples, oranges, grapes, and many others. He stopped a lady who was going by and asked her to explain all of this to him. He learned from her that in this dimension, everything was about the Christmas spirit. *I am surely going to spread the Christmas spirit,* he thought to himself. As he looked across the street, he saw candy cane cars flying through the air. Jason crossed over to the other side of the street.

A short distance away, there was another street named Present Street. He noticed that everything on this street was wrapped in beautiful paper and ribbons. He decided to take a closer look. He found that one of the gifts had his name on it. He opened it. Inside was a beautiful pair of gloves. Jason began talking to a man he met. He asked him to tell him more about this dimension. The man told him to come with him. They walked further down the street until they came to another street Cookie Street. The delicious smell coming from the street was making him hungry.

They continued on to Candy Cane Lane, where many people were getting ready to have a race in their flying cars. Jason sat down to watch the race. What a sight it was: nine candy cane cars flying through tunnels of beautiful white snow. He told the man next to him he thought it was magnificent. He gave him a gingerbread cookie and some fine hot cocoa.

After the race Jason left to find the reindeer. When he did, he greeted them. They began to shake their heads back and forth. He saw Saint Nick and inquired about what their names were. The kind, old gentleman told Jason that before he left, he would know what all of their names were. "What is really important," Saint Nick said, "is the children."

Jason agreed. Christmas, for children, was a time of joy and smiles. "I am starting to understand the glory of Christmas," Jason told Saint Nick.

"Good, that is very good," Nick said to Jason. Then he told Jason that he wanted him to continue his exploration because there was still more to see.

"It is very colorful here, and the people are always happy," Jason said as he turned to Saint Nick. Saint Nick only laughed and said he would see him later on. As he walked, he noticed how happy the children were with all of their gifts. Then he noticed a big, bright red house. He commented on what a nice house it was and walked up to it. When he went inside, he saw a beautiful painting of Saint Nick. Above the painting were the words *Santa Claus.* He also saw a beautiful pipe collection and lots of toys. He opened a closet and saw that it was full of red suits edged with white fur. Jason thought to himself that these suits could make a man bold.

Saint Nick walked in, and Jason asked him to tell him more about what he wanted him to learn. So Saint Nick told Jason what he shall be called and how he should present it to the people. Then he told him that there was one more sight he must see and that he must remember it well. Jason went outside and saw lots of people gathering around a big pine tree and placing presents underneath it and between its branches. He saw a couple of children trying to get their presents higher up in the tree. He went over to the children and lifted them up. He was happy to do it. Jason asked some of the people to tell him more about what they were doing because he needed to learn about if for the children of his dimension.

Jason walked back over to where Saint Nick was. Saint Nick told him that it was time for him to go home. "Oh, one more thing, Jason!" Nick said to him. "The reindeer have a present for you!"

Jason and Saint Nick climbed into the sleigh and waved to all the people who were standing by and waving and calling "good-bye" to them.

"Go ahead," Nick said to Jason. "You say it."

Jason smiled and yelled, "Hot cocoa!"

The reindeer took off in a hurry. Jason decided to open his present from the reindeer. Inside were eight mugs, each with one of the reindeer's names on it. There was also a recipe for hot cocoa. As they went through the whirlwind of colors, Jason turned around and waved to the people again.

Dedicated to the spirit of Christmas. May it live on.

Storytellers

Far away in another universe, a world half the size of Earth was named Stories. The people who live there were famous for their incredible storytelling abilities. Their assignment was to travel to other worlds to tell their stories. One woman, the master storyteller, began to tell stories. She calls Jonah, her best storyteller, and told him to be ready to go to Earth and tell his stories to children. "Yes, Master," Jonah replied.

"Well, as soon as the sun sets, you must go to your destination," she told him.

As the sun set, Jonah entered a chamber that turned him into a colorful crystal and left like a shooting star to Earth. Five more storytellers left the same time for other assignments. As Jonah landed on Earth in Boston, Massachusetts in 1921, he changed back to his human body. Jonah walked up the street and said "hello" to everybody he met. He stopped one man. "Sir can you point out a park?"

"Sure," said the man. "Walk three blocks straight, make a left and go two more blocks."

"Thank you, sir," Jonah told the man. When Jonah arrived at the park he saw a lot of children playing. He pointed his finger, and a tent and organ appeared. The tent was emblazoned with "The Storyteller." Suddenly music started playing. All the children came running over, and Jonah asked them, "Would you kids like to hear some stories?"

"Yes,yes," the children shouted. "All right, gather around me and sit down on the grass and relax," Jonah said. "Now once upon a time there was a world called Myth, and there lived a king who was very, very sad."

One kid asked, "Why was he sad?"

"Listen to the story," Jonah said, "and you will find out. Atlas the dragon, who lives among the people, has a bad bad toothache, and he is driving everybody crazy. You see, everybody in the kingdom loves Atlas." Jonah tells the kids. "But the king's knights are getting nowhere. The dragon keeps blowing them away with his breath. At night you can hear the dragon in pain. The king has bitten his nails left and right and is worried that the dragon will take out his pain on the people.

"So a boy named Henry tells the king, 'I will pull out the dragon's tooth.'

"The king looks at the boy, 'You my son?'

"'Yes, me, my lord.'

"The king sits back and tells the boy, 'Let me think in this.' After a few minutes, he answered, 'Well, okay, son, go ahead. Nobody has gone to sleep in days because of that tooth.'

"The boy leaves, and he has a long strong rope to take with him. As the boy enters Atlas's domain, he sees everything is burnt from the dragon's madness of his tooth. Atlas sees the boy and says, 'What are you doing here, boy?'

"'I came to pull out your tooth.'

"'You!' said the dragon.

"'Yes, me, says the boy. 'Now when I count to three, you fly, and maybe your tooth will come out.' As the boy counts to three the dragon takes off and the tooth comes out! As the tooth falls to the ground, Henry says, 'That is a big, big tooth!'"The dragon is so happy that he flies around in circles, blowing fire out his nose. As he lands, he asks the boy if he wants to go for a ride. 'Yes, yes, I would love that!' Henry exclaims. "So the dragon picks up the boy with his mouth and pulls him onto his back. The dragon tells the boy to count to three. Henry starts counting, and they start flying all around the countryside. The people look up and they are so happy. Now they can get some sleep. As they get to the palace, the dragon lands, and the king comes running out all happy again.

"Atlas says, 'Well, I will go to the other side of the world and look for a female dragon named Misty.'

"As the people watch the dragon fly away, the king turns to Henry. 'My son, you earned knighthood. Let it be known throughout the kingdom that you will be Sir Henry.'

"Okay, kids, did you like that?"

All the kids were shouting, 'Tell us more!' Even some adults were listening to the stories.

As Jonah looked at the children, he saw a boy who looked very sad sitting by himself. Jonah shook his head. "Okay, kids, here is the next story. This story is about a world of cartoons.

"Once upon a time there was a world called Tools. They have outdone themselves, and there is no more room on their world to build. The master toolmaker is a hammer of gold, the other tools are silver. The master tells them, 'We will build space rides to go to other worlds and build on them.' So they start to build, and each one is a giant bricklayer's hammer. You see, tools are always working. They have no sense of time. As the master tool tells them what world to go to, all the tools start entering their rides–five in total. They set course for the planet Earth, thousands of years before humans. As they reach Earth, each ride goes its own way–to China, to Russia, to the United States, to Europe, and to the Middle East. In China they start building tunnels and houses all around the countryside. They fashion marble buildings and little towns, one after another.

One kid says, "They are fast workers!"

"Oh, yes," Jonah says, "very fast. The tools that go to Russia start building houses made of rock and tunnels that go from one valley to another valley. They build tools of themselves standing a hundred feet high. In Europe they build dams everywhere."

One boy says to Jonah, "They like to build all the time!"

Jonah says, "that is what they do. In the Middle East they are building roads and bridges everywhere. If they aren't near a bridge they build one anyway. In the United States they are building rivers, lakes, and canals everywhere. They build tools like themselves from coast to coast. The master tool calls them back, and they go back to their world called Tools.

Jonah asked the children, "did you like that story?"

"Oh yes!" all the kids shout. Even more adults were shouting, "More stories!"

Jonah looked at the boy who was sad and put his hand over his mouth and thought. "Okay, one more story, and then I have to go. This is a cartoon story also.

"Once upon a time there were five worlds two miles apart from each other, but the main world was at the center. They were called the world of instruments. Over the years they travel in space guitar ships, and they also send out a triangle which collects music from all over the universe. They take turns playing concerts for each other's worlds. On the center world they are always cleaning their instruments because they want them to look good. There is always some kind of orchestra playing music on the main instrument world. There are four speakers a mile high on the center world so everybody in the other worlds can hear the music. They are always trying to outdo themselves to see who can give the best concert. Now they are getting ready to have a major event. One triangle that they sent out to collect music came back with something good from Earth, written by a man named Beethoven."

Jonah said, "Raise your hand if you have heard of Beethoven." He was impressed most of the hands were up—especially the older people.

"the concert begins as the harp, cello, viola, violin, trumpet, trombone, flute, clarinet, the piano, and the triangle play. You can see the music notes just floating to the other four small worlds. When the concert is over, all the instruments from all the worlds begin playing at the same time. When there is a good concert, they all do that to show greatness in music. The instrument worlds sent out a triangle again to collect more music.

"Okay, kids," said Jonah, "it is getting late. Be careful going home. I will be back next year with more stories." Jonah noticed the boy who was sad was still sitting down. Jonah walked over and said, "Hello, son. What is wrong?"

The boy said, "Oh, nothing."

Jonah put his hand on his head and said, "I see what is on your mind." He pointed his finger at the tent and organ, and they disappeared. "What is your name, son? Wait, wait, I know. Tom, right?

"Yes," the boy said. "How did you know?"

"Okay, Tom, would you like to come with me?"

"Yes, sir."

"No, call me Jonah. Jonah."

"Yes, Jonah."

"I want you to take my hand." As Jonah and Tom joined hands, they turned into a colorful crystal and left like shooting stars to the world of stories.

The Symbol

Jeff Waters drove down the road with his pal, a husky named Treasure. As he was driving, a woman came running out of her house and stopped Jeff. He got out of the car and asked, "What is wrong here.

"My house is on fire! And my baby is up there."

Jeff went to the back of the car and got some rope. "Let's go, Treasure."

As they entered the house, the fire was so bad that as he and Treasure went up stairs, pieces of the cellar fell and hit Jeff in the back. He fell to one knee but started up the stairs again. Treasure started barking, and Jeff saw the baby. He tied a rope around the baby and started lowering the baby down.

Meanwhile, the fire department arrived, so Jeff and Treasure started down the stairs, and the whole house started to fall. By the time the firemen got in, it was too late to rescue Jeff and Treasure. The police were outside, and one police officer said, "It is a shame. The man has nobody to call. I guess the dog was his friend."

At the wake three people showed up, and one was a priest who said, "Jeff and Treasure will be in that woman's heart forever."

At the gates of heaven he and his husky walked up to two large pillars, and an angel came to stand between them. The angel said, "We saw what you have done, and that was real good. That was very good."

Jeff said, "but where am I?"

"Heaven," said the angel, "but now, Jeff, you must go back to Earth to earn your halo. You have already received your wings, both of you."

So Jeff and Treasure landed back on Earth, and their wings disappeared. They came near a house and heard a woman talking to her son. He looked at Treasure, and it seemed that he and his mother were having hard times. Jeff got in front of the door and knocked without touching the door. As the woman opened the door, Jeff stuck out his hand. The woman seemed friendly. "Hi there," Jeff said. "Could I buy some food for me and my dog?"

"Yes," the woman said. "Come in. Been on the road long?"

"Oh, not that long."

"That is a beautiful husky you got there," said the woman.

"That is Treasure."

"Treasure," she said. "That is nice."

"I am Jeff, and who are you?"

"My name is Judy, and my son is John."

Jeff asked her if she was a farmer, and she replied, "Yes, but it is hard. We need somebody to help us.

"Where is your husband?" Jeff asked.

"He left five years ago." Jeff shook his head.

"Hey, mister," said the boy, "can I play with your dog?"

"Sure," Jeff said. They spent two hours there, and then Jeff said, "I have got to go. Good luck! Something good will happen."

As they got to town, Treasure saw a dog and cat ready to go at it, so Treasure picked up one of his paws, and the cat began showing her perfection to the dog. Jeff looked down. "Good boy." As they walked, they heard a man talking to another man about a farmer. The man said, I know a lot about farming, but I need to get my own within hours."

Judy drove by at just that moment and got a flat tire, so Jeff raised his hand and the man, Frank, went to help her, and they started talking. Soon the man got in the car with Judy and drove off. Jeff looked at Treasure and said, "Well, good things are going to happen between them." Their wings started to appear as they disappeared in the mist.

In Africa a small native boy prepared to hike around the countryside. His father told him, "Be careful and don't go too far. There are still a lot of wild animals out there."

"Okay, Dad, I will be careful."

As the boy wandered deeper and deeper into the jungle, he realized that he was lost. He heard all kinds of noises coming from the jungle, and he started to run but fell in a ditch and could not get out. Meanwhile, a tiger was preying around and saw the boy. all of a sudden Jeff and Treasure appeared. As their wings disappeared, Treasure put out his paw, and the tiger became as tame as a kitten. Jeff walked over to the tiger. "Okay, boy, go ahead. Go on your way."

Jeff reached down and pulled the boy up. "You have got to be more careful, son," he said. They left the jungle and returned the boy to his tribe. The boy told his father what happened, and the father thanked Jeff. He invited Jeff and Treasure to stay for dinner.

Jeff replied, "yes, I would love that!"

Meanwhile the boy was having some fun with Treasure. The father turned to Jeff and asked, "Who are you?"

Jeff said, "Don't worry about me. The main thing is your boy is safe." Jeff told the father, "I need to leave now," so the father gave Jeff a strong handshake.

The boy followed them as they were leaving and watched in shock as he saw wings appear on Jeff and Treasure as they disappeared. The boy just stood there looking at the sky.

In Montana a group of Boy Scouts prepared for a two-day hike. The scout master was making sure that they had all the necessary camping needs and food. In the woods the scout master told the boys about the trees and how old they were, about stalking, camping, poisonous plants, and all kinds of things about nature. They got to a cave, and the scout master says, "this looks like a good place to camp." He looked in the cave. "Okay, boys, let's make camp inside the cave!" So the boys made their beds, and the scout master built a campfire. When they finished their meals around the camp-fire, the scout master begins telling them a story.

All of a sudden a bear came in front of the cave and the scout master pushed the boys on top of the rocks so the bear couldn't reach them. The bear was about forty feet from the scout master when Jeff and Treasure appeared in front of the cave. Jeff put out his hand, and the bear came over to him and started licking his hand, so Jeff sent the bear on his way. The boys and their scout master are amazed. "All right, boys, you can come down now," the scout master called. They all got down and surrounded Jeff and Treasure and started thanking them.

The scout master said, "I have never seen anything like it. You must be real good with animals." Jeff and Treasure join them around the campfire. The scout master starts telling them a campfire story to help them settle down. Jeff and Treasure walked out of the cave and into the woods.

All of a sudden a voice said, "Okay, Jeff, it is time for you to come back." As Jeff and Treasure got to the gates of heaven, they opened up, and the man and his dog started walking between rows of angels as the angels bowed their heads. Jeff's and Treasure's wings and halos appeared as they walked. Jeff heard music and to his astonishment saw Harpo Marx playing his harp. Harpo looked at him and started slapping his leg like he wanted Jeff to sit on his lap. Jeff thought to himself, *Just like his movie*. As Jeff and Treasure reached the head angel, the angel said, "Jeff, you and Treasure were outstanding. You will be the angel of children, so if you like you could go back to Earth to carry on good deeds. This is your gift; this is what you do best. so Jeff and Treasure reappeared on Earth, walking down a country road as their wings and halo once again disappeared.

Candy World: The Return
of Lou and Greta

Professor Twinkle was just about the meanest bug in the world. For years he had tried to sell his candy formula to candy tycoons, but they didn't want to be bothered. They knew he was a no-good scoundrel.

So the professor made plans with his gang called the Tutti-Fruitti Boys, who all had to wear pullover sweaters in different colors. His plan was to hit every gum ball plant and steal all of the gum balls in the world.

Lou and Greta were just returning home from their vacation. Greta was looking out of the airplane window chewing her Juicy Fruits, while Lou was looking at the prize he got out of his Cracker Jacks. All of a sudden, two men started causing a lot of trouble on the airplane, so Lou got up and beat them silly. "What a man my Lou is," Greta said as all of the people on the plane cheered for Lou.

Lou rested his hand on the door of the airplane and accidentally opened it. He fell right out of the door. Luckily he saw a big balloon down on the ground. He put his hands on his cheeks to guide his landing. He landed right on the balloon and bounced off, landing beside an ice cream truck. "Do you have any Cracker Jacks?" Lou asked the ice cream man.

"Just ice cream, buddy," the man told him.

Meanwhile, five cargo planes flew over Yankee Stadium and dropped all of the stolen gum balls onto the field during the game. There were so many gum balls that they piled up two feet above the stadium.

At the same time Lou had gone to the airport to wait for Greta. As soon as she saw Lou, she ran up to him and started kissing him all over his face. "Lou," she said, "I was worried!"

"Wait a second," Lou said as he reached up and pulled a Juicy Fruit off of his face.

Then he looked at Greta and said, "Let's go home."

When they got home Greta found a note. "Oh, Lou, the boys have gone out to a cartoon convention," Greta said to him.

Lou just said, "Greta, where are the Cracker Jacks?" as he flipped on the television. Then he said, "I think there is somebody here!"

Lou got up and walked over to the kitchen door. Before he reached to open it, the door opened and sent Lou flying across the room. "Hi, how are you doing? My name is Wally. You know your grandmother always invited me over."

Lou got up and rubbed his head. "Yeah, how are you doing?" he said to him.

All of a sudden there was a new flash on the television. Professor Twinkle and his Tutti-Fruity Boys had melted all of the Hershey's chocolate in Hershey, Pennsylvania with some kind of ray gun, and the town was covered in Hershey's chocolate.

"The Cracker Jacks' plant is next," Wally said.

Lou stood up and said, "Not if Wally and me are waiting for them!" Lou looked at Greta and thought to himself that she had better stop eating so many Juicy Fruits because they were going to her head.

Wally and Lou left for the candy factory. When they got there, Lou couldn't keep his hands off the Cracker Jacks.

"Easy, Lou," Wally said to him. "Save some for the customers!"

Just then, Lou heard something. "Hear that?" he said to Wally. "Let's hide!"

Around the corner came five Tutti-Fruity Boys. "I will take those three, and you take the others," Wally said to Lou.

As the Tutti-Fruity Boys began to destroy the plant, out came Wally. He was boxing and hitting them left and right. He was so fast that they didn't even see the punches coming.

70

Meanwhile, Lou had the other two in headlocks and was banging their heads together. "find some rope!" Wally said to Lou.

They tied the boys up with the rope, called the police, and then left. When they got home, Greta told them that it had been on T.V. The police had captured the Tutti-Fruity Boys. "I know. I was there, remember? See me on T.V. eating Cracker Jacks?" Lou said. Then he turned to Wally and said, "You're lucky that they can't see you."

"That's right. Except the Tutti-Fruity Boys saw me," Wally said.

"Why?" Lou asked.

"Because I let them see me, so that they would know who was beating them up."

Meanwhile, Professor Twinkle was steaming. He was stomping all over the place, throwing anything he could find at his men.

Back with Lou, Greta asked, "You boys hungry?"

"Yes," said Lou and Wally.

"Then I'll make some sandwiches." she said.

"You got a good woman, there," Wally said to Lou, "but her mind can lose it." Then he said to Lou, "Tomorrow we check the M&M's plant. I have a feeling."

So the next day, when the boys were ready to leave, Greta gave Lou a big kiss. As Lou and Wally were walking out of the house, Wally said, "Lou, you have a Juicy Fruit on your face."

"I don't believe that woman!" Lou said.

At home Greta was reading a book when her squirrel friend Strawberry came out.

"Where are your father and sister?" Greta asked her.

"They went to the cartoon convention, but I wanted to spend some time with you," Strawberry said.

"Come sit next to me," Greta said to her. Just then, the front door broke down and three of the professor's boys came in and kidnapped Greta. Strawberry said to herself that she was glad that they couldn't see her. Then she realized that she had to find Lou and Wally.

At the M&M's plant Lou and Wally were waiting. Lou said to Wally, "Are you going to eat all of those M&M's?"

"They're good. And look, they don't melt in your hand," Wally said.

"Yeah, yeah, yeah," said Lou.

All of a sudden, seven Tutti-Fruity Boys broke into the plant with axes. Lou jumped down on them. Wally came out and started showing them a boxing event. He got a hold of one as he was punching two others with crazy speed. Lou had two of them in headlocks and was jumping up and down. Wally was hitting them so hard that they were flying through walls. Lou was running with the two men he had in headlocks and crashing them into walls. When it was all over, Lou said to Wally, "See—not one M&M was damaged except for the ones you ate."

Just then Strawberry came running in and told Lou and Wally what had happened to Greta. They hurried home to wait to hear from the professor. Wally turned to Lou and said, "Don't worry, Lou. We'll get her back."

Then the telephone rang, and Professor Twinkle told them where they were.

"You stay here," Lou said to Strawberry. "I've got some peanuts in the kitchen. That's what squirrels eat, right?"

"No, Lou. I want Cracker Jacks!" she told him.

So Lou and Wally left. Lou turned to Wally and said, "They have her at the Juicy Fruits factory."

"There will be a lot of them, Lou."

"We'll take care of them," Lou said.

At the plant the professor had Greta tied up and hanging above a big vat of syrup used to make Juicy Fruits. The Tutti-Fruitti Boys were hiding all around. "My Lou will fix you for this!" Greta yelled.

As Lou and Wally got there, Wally said, "I'll go around back, and you go through the front. Be careful, Lou."

Lou turned to Wally and said, "No problem. I am Lou Wind!" Lou went around back to where the guards were. They had been knocked unconscious and were tied up. Lou went up to two of the professor's men and tapped them on their shoulders. Then he smashed their heads together. Wally rushed in through the front and was hopping all over hitting them with his speed. Half of the boys didn't know where they were because they were hit so hard. Lou saw a rope hanging, so he got the rope and took off like Tarzan, kicking the boys at the same time. Four boys got around Lou just as he saw Greta hanging over the vat. He was really getting mad now. All four of the boys jumped on Lou at the same time, but Lou beat them silly. Wally was watching with a smile and saying, "That's it, Lou. Hit him again. Now go for the big punch!"

With one punch, Lou knocked out the four boys. Just then Professor Twinkle started to lower Greta.

"Lou!" Greta yelled out. Then Wally did an incredible jump and got Greta down. The professor started to run, but Lou was right on him.

"Don't hit me, Lou!" the professor begged.

"All right," said Lou, "let's go."

So Lou and Wally tied them up and called the police.

"I will see you at home," said Wally.

Greta really started really kidding Lou. "I was worried!"

When the police arrived they were all cheering for Lou.

"Hey Lou, you have something on your face!" Lou looked at Greta and shook his head.

When they got home, Strawberry was so happy to see Greta. "I have to go now," she told them.

"Say hello to your father," Lou told her.

"Okay, Lou."

"Wait here, I've got some Cracker Jacks for you and your sister."

Then Wally said, "I think I'll go to the cartoon convention."

Lou sat down, and Greta sat on his lap and said, "Lou, you will always be my man!"

"Look what I got out of my Cracker Jacks. It's a small comic book!" Lou said.

Greta just looked up and said, "What a man my Lou is!"

Leo the Lion: The Destiny of Leo

In Hawaii John and Kim were taking in the sun at a beach in Maui. It was early in the morning, so there was only a handful of people. John and Kim enjoyed the sun, and they came to the beach whenever they could. "You know, you never did tell me how it was spending years in the stars," Kim said, turning to John.

"It was beautiful. Maybe some day I'll take you there with Leo," John told her. Then all of a sudden, his eyes began to glow with pure yellow light. He sensed danger somewhere nearby. He looked out at the ocean and saw children swimming and having fun. Then he saw a shark swimming toward them. He jumped up and started to run toward the ocean as he rubbed his ring and said, "Leo."

Leo dived into the ocean after the shark. It was amazing the way he could do the butterfly stroke. Passing the children Leo grabbed ahold of the shark with his paws and lifted it out of the water and threw it as far as the naked eye could see.

Leo swam back and hid before he turned back into John. When he got back over to where Kim was, she said to him, "I couldn't be more proud of you, John," and John's eyes glowed with pure yellow light.

Back at the hotel, people were talking about Leo and what he had done. "I would love to get my paws on him if I could find out who he is!" said one woman.

At dinner, Kim could not help looking at John with love in her eyes, and John was the same way. After they finished dinner, they went up to their room. Kim put her arms around John, and his eyes shined the yellow light.

The next day, on an airplane to California, Kim said to John, "Let's go to Disneyland!"

"Sure," said John. "I've never been there before. It sounds like fun."

When they got to Disneyland, they checked into the Disney Hotel. "When we get there, let's go on all of the rides!" Kim said happily.

"You bet!" said John. "Maybe even twice." Kim threw him a big smile.

On the Dumbo ride Kim said to John, "That's a crazy hat you've got on!" as she touched his goofy hat.

"Yours is just as crazy!" John said to her, laughing.

"Hey, look! It's the president and his family!" Kim said, pointing to where they were.

"Even with all of the Secret Service men there, they're taking a chance," John said as his eyes began to glow yellow.

After the Dumbo ride ended, they went into the haunted house. John's hearing was so acute that he could hear men talking above them. "Everybody is ready. We will wait until he is close to Tom Sawyer Island, and then we'll kill him!" one of the men said. John told Kim what he had just heard. Then he got out of the ride, and since it was dark and nobody could see him, he changed into Leo.

Just as the beautiful lion reached the entrance, a shot was fired, and the president's son was hit. The Secret Service men were running all over the place, and the president was on his knees next to his son, crying.

Leo caught one of the guys and threw him in a lake. He grabbed another and looked him right in the eyes with the most terrifying face before slapping him and sending him flying into a popcorn stand. The Secret Service men got him after that.

Leo went over to the president's son and picked him up. A bright yellow light came out of his eyes and went right into the boy's gunshot wound. Within minutes the boy opened his eyes.

When Leo got to Bear Mountain, he changed back into John. Kim was waiting for him there. "John, you have the power to heal also?" she asked in awe.

"I never knew that I had that power. I just knew I was angry and I had to do something," John told her.

"Well, whatever you did, it worked!" Kim said with a slight laugh.

On the news, word had gotten out about what the people had witnessed at Disneyland.

Back home in New York John and Kim were watching the news when a special report came on. The president was making a speech. "I don't know who this person is, but what he has done is something I will never forget," said the president, wiping tears from his eyes. "I would love to meet him face-to-face in the White House, if that is possible," he continued. Then he looked into the camera and said, "If you're watching, I hope that someday we can meet."

John stood up and turned off the television. He looked at Kim. "Well, what do you think?" he asked her.

"Yes, you should see him," she said, "but see him as Leo and not as John."

"You're right," John told her. "If I saw him as myself, I would be putting you in harm's way. Okay, I'll go on Monday."

"Great. Now, how about a picnic tomorrow since it will be Sunday?"

"Sounds good," said John.

The next day in Central Park John and Kim were enjoying the warm spring sun. As Kim poured a glass of wine for John, she said, "It would be nice to have children, John."

"Perhaps someday we will," John told her.

Other people in the park were also having fun. Children were playing all kinds of games, and Kim and John watched with happiness.

Meanwhile a gang was walking through the park, stealing people's food and using all kinds of bad language. "It's a shame the way kids are becoming," John said to Kim.

Some of the kids in the gang stole a ball that some young children were playing with. some of the kids started to cry. The gang member who had the ball threw it really hard at a baby carriage. The carriage started to roll down a hill.

"I'd like to see one day of peace!" John said to Kim, just before jumping up and turning into Leo.

As Leo ran after the carriage, the baby's mother was right behind him. He caught the carriage and handed the baby to her. She smiled at him and said, "thank you!"

Leo turned around with his eyes really glowing and went after the gang. He got them cornered, but instead of doing anything to them, he just looked at them like he wanted to give them a good beating. Then with his paw he pointed to the park exit. He had never seen anyone run as fast as those kids did. They were trying to get away so fast that they kept running into each other.

The people in the park clapped their hands for Leo as he disappeared in the park.

The next day John took an early flight to Washington, D. C. Kim stayed home to do some remodeling on the house that she had wanted to do.

As John passed through the gates to the White House, he looked around to make sure that nobody was watching him. Then he transformed into Leo. He jumped right over the gates and landed on the front lawn. All of the Secret Service men saw him and ran out to greet him. As Leo entered the White House, the president asked him, "Would you like to be alone with me?"

Leo nodded, so they went to the Oval Office. Once they were there, Leo changed back to John.

"I'm very pleased to meet you," the president said to him. "What you did for my son at Disneyland, well, I will always be grateful to you for that."

"I am just happy that I was there, or else . . . well, you know."

"Yes, I do know," the president said. "John, tell me how this happened."

After two hours John told the president the whole story. After John shook the president's hand again and left, the president forgot all that had happened because John had discovered that Leo had the power to make people forget things they had seen.

Later, when John got home, he gave Kim a big hug, then he turned on the television. A special report was on, detailing an impending accident. A train was running out of control and was rushing into New York.

"They will need my help!" John said to Kim as he turned into Leo and leaped out of the window. As he got to the entrance of the train and headed down the stairs, he saw the police guiding people up the ramp to safety before the train got there. Leo dived down onto the tracks and started to run at an incredible speed until he got to the back of the train. He grabbed hold of the train with his mighty paws and held onto it. Gradually it slowed down and came to a stop. He ripped the door open. One man aboard was having a mild heart attack. Leo made way for the paramedics to help him.

When John got home, Kim said that she had seen everything. It had been all over the news. The mayor said that from that day forward, they would celebrate Leo on that day.

"It's quite an honor, John," she said.

"I'm just glad that nobody was hurt," John said. Then they decided to out to dinner and see a movie.

A week later, John asked Kim if she would like to live at their home in New York half of the year and spend the other half in Oregon. "That would be nice, John. A little country, a little city," Kim said.

"Okay, but first there is something I want to show you," John told her.

John changed into Leo and held Kim's hand with his paw. Then they both turned into stars and left for the heavens like shooting stars.